MYSTERY OF THE MISSING MOTHER

"Kellach. Come at once." Driskoll bent forward to catch his breath, hands pressed to his thighs.

"What is it?" Kellach asked. "Did you two run all the way here?" He'd never seen his brother's eyes shine with such excitement.

"You're not going to believe this," Driskoll said. "Even I didn't believe it at first. I mean, how could it be? But it is. It's really true."

"What are you going on about? What's really true?" Kellach glanced from Moyra to Driskoll.

"It's Mom," Driskoll said. "I've found her. She's back."

THE SILVER SPELL

ANJALI BANERJEE

KNIGHTS OF THE SILVER DRAGON

BOOK 8

COVER & INTERIOR ART
EMILY FIEGENSCHUH

MIRROR
STONE

The Silver Spell

©2005 Wizards of the Coast, Inc.

Distributed in the United States by Holtzbrinck Publishing. Distributed in Canada by Fenn Ltd.

Distributed to the hobby, toy, and comic trade in the United States and Canada by regional distributors.

Distributed worldwide by Wizards of the Coast, Inc. and regional distributors.

Printed in the U.S.A.

Cover and interior art by Emily Fiegenschuh
Cartography by Dennis Kauth
First Printing: August 2005
Library of Congress Catalog Card Number: 2004116906

9 8 7 6 5 4 3 2 1

US ISBN: 0-7869-3750-5
ISBN-13: 978-0-7869-3750-9
620-88980000-001-EN

U.S., CANADA,
ASIA, PACIFIC, & LATIN AMERICA
Wizards of the Coast, Inc.
P.O. Box 707
Renton, WA 98057-0707
+1-800-324-6496

EUROPEAN HEADQUARTERS
Hasbro UK Ltd
Caswell Way
Newport, Gwent NP9 0YH
GREAT BRITAIN
Please keep this address for your records

Visit our web site at **www.mirrorstonebooks.com**

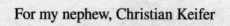
For my nephew, Christian Keifer

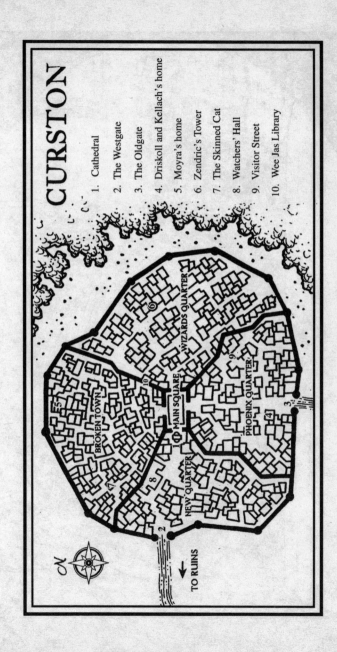

CURSTON

1. Cathedral
2. The Westgate
3. The Oldgate
4. Driskoll and Kellach's home
5. Moyra's home
6. Zendric's Tower
7. The Skinned Cat
8. Watchers' Hall
9. Visitor Street
10. Wee Jas Library

N

TO RUINS

BROKEN TOWN

WIZARDS' QUARTER

MAIN SQUARE

NEW QUARTER

PHOENIX QUARTER

CHAPTER

1

Kellach focused on the blank stone wall and chanted the spell. He imagined a red door with a lion's head knocker.

Nothing happened.

Torchlight flickered across the wall's textured surface. Kellach could hear Zendric breathing, smell the musty odor of the wizard's robes.

"Concentrate, boy." The old wizard tapped the floor with his staff. "No distractions. Push away all other thoughts."

"I'm trying." Kellach tried to ignore the noise out in the Wizards' Quarter. It felt as though the whole city clamored inside his brain.

"Picture the door. Focus. One day your life may depend on it, boy."

I'm not a boy, Kellach thought. He gritted his teeth. Sweat broke out on his forehead.

He figured at fourteen, he should count as a man, but Zendric still saw him as a gangly teenager, an apprentice in need of instruction. Well, Kellach would show him.

His mind burned an image into stone. Then, with a great groan, a section of the wall swirled, melted, and hardened into a red door.

There was a faint burning smell, and Kellach's heart sank. What had gone wrong?

Zendric frowned. "Not bad, if you want a mouse door."

Kellach's cheeks heated. "I don't understand. I thought of a regular-sized door!"

Zendric shook his head. "One of a wizard's greatest assets is patience. You must take your time and think big!"

"But I tried—"

The mouse door faded and became part of the wall again.

"Spells require practice and dedication," Zendric said.

Kellach bit his lip. "I should've pictured a door the height of this tower."

"We'll try another spell." Zendric strode to the bookshelves and pulled out a thick, velvet-bound spellbook. He opened to a page in the middle. Dust flew, and Zendric coughed. "Here, Voice Alteration."

First, Kellach learned to mimic his friend Moyra's high, melodic voice with a hint of wind chimes.

"Kellach, stop teasing me. You are SO annoying." His throat tingled afterward.

Zendric clapped. "Excellent. Moyra will be pleased."

Kellach broke into a smile. Warmth spread through his chest. He could have fun with that spell.

Next, Kellach tried his brother's deeper, raspy voice. At

twelve, Driskoll's voice was changing. "Don't trip over the sleeping gnomes, Kellach."

"Bravo! You're a natural." Zendric tapped the floor again. Tall and stately, he exuded the quiet authority of a wise elf.

"I can't wait to try—" Kellach's voice came out a raspy whisper. He pressed his fingers to his throat. "What happened, Zendric?"

"You've gone hoarse—a temporary condition. Voice alteration drains you, so use it sparingly, or you may lose your voice altogether. No practical jokes."

"Of course not. Why would I do that?" Kellach whispered.

"Last spell for today," Zendric said. "The secret page spell. For this one, use your mother's spellbook."

Kellach pulled the thin volume from his pack. Holding the spellbook brought a lump to his throat. It was all he had left of his mother Jourdain. It was a simple memento from her childhood, before she became a full-fledged wizard. Kellach had often leafed through the book, hoping it held the key to what had become of her five years ago. The slanted handwriting never yielded a clue.

In the years following Jourdain's disappearance, Kellach's imagination had run wild—she'd been kidnapped by an evil sorcerer or taken hostage by a gang of goblins. He'd often woken in a sweat after a horrific nightmare in which his mother's lifeless body floated in a river of blood.

As time passed, the nightmares faded, and Jourdain's face blurred in his memory. He felt vaguely guilty, as if he'd somehow forgotten her, so he consciously conjured her in his mind,

3

keeping her alive. Sometimes late at night, he imagined her standing next to him, whispering his name.

He hoped that when she'd disappeared, she'd gone to a beautiful place where the sparrows sang and the sun shone through a clear sky. A safe place, unlike Curston. A place without monsters.

"Stop daydreaming, boy. Choose a page. The secret page spell will render the words illegible."

"Ah, I see. Like an obscuring spell."

"Similar. To the untrained eye, the letters will appear to be mere symbols. Use this spell when you want to—"

"Hide something precious. I know." Kellach flipped through the spellbook past a page written in silver ink so metallic that his own fragmented reflection shimmered in the letters. Though he could not decipher the language, he called it the mirror spell. The silver had not faded over the years. He liked that page too much to hide it. He flipped farther into the book and stopped on page 32.

He began to recite the secret page spell.

His tongue tied itself in knots. "Is anything happening? The page looks the same."

"Keep trying," Zendric said sternly. He strode to the window, pushed open the panes, and brought back a falcon perched on his forearm. The bird's silvery plumage gleamed in the torchlight. As the long wings folded, Kellach heard the faint whir and click of gears. A clockwork falcon! A machine that moved with smooth, mechanical precision.

Kellach let out a long breath. He'd never seen a contraption that looked so real. The metallic feathers were delicately crafted, and the head was painted with dramatic pink and blue markings.

The falcon's piercing, black eyes blinked.

A palpable presence seeped into Kellach's bones. He pictured large wings, black and bony. They weren't the falcon's wings— they belonged to something evil. He shook his head to dispel the image.

Zendric bent his head, putting his ear to the creature's feathery face. "What's that you say? Slow down so I can understand."

"The bird talks?" Kellach rushed over, with his mother's open spellbook still in his hands.

"Jabbers more like it. Something about Ssarine."

"The medusa? What about her?"

"She's ill."

"Ill with what?"

"I don't know. All I know is that she needs my help. She would not ask if she didn't. I must go."

Zendric reached out the window, and the falcon spread its magnificent clockwork wings and flapped away.

"You're leaving right now? But the secret page spell—"

"Keep practicing. Show me when I return." Zendric hastily crammed a few vials, books, and instruments into a pack. A hunk of cheese, a loaf of bread, and a bladder of water levitated from a table and dropped inside. An extra set of wizard's robes followed, floating through the air. "I hope I haven't forgotten anything."

5

"When will you be back?"

"When I know Ssarine is well." Zendric drew a white circle on the floor with the end of his staff, then poured amber dust to cover the area of the circle.

Kellach sneezed as a cloud of dust kicked up. "You're teleporting to Medusa Island?"

"The island's far, and I must make haste." Zendric hoisted the pack over his shoulder and stepped into the circle. "Take care, boy. Watch over the city while I'm away."

"But—"

"No arguments." Zendric winked, then he was gone.

A moment later, the circle disappeared too, leaving only a powdery residue.

"Wait!" Kellach shouted. His voice echoed back at him.

He hoped Ssarine would recover quickly. Although the watchers protected the city, Curston felt darker, colder, and more perilous without its great wizard. Kellach could almost hear the monsters whispering, conspiring as they crouched in the shadows. It was hard to believe Curston had once been called Promise.

Five years ago, a group of treasure hunters had broken a seal deep in the ruins a few miles outside the city, releasing a multitude of demons and depraved creatures. Ever since, the residents were always on watch for the evil beasts bent on destroying Curston.

A shiver climbed Kellach's back, but he shook away the fear. He was a Knight of the Silver Dragon, and Knights didn't get scared. Zendric had asked him to watch over the city, and he, Driskoll, and Moyra would do just that.

The everburning torches dimmed, and the chamber grew large and lonely. The worktables and writing desks seemed to shift in the darkness. The wall tapestries seemed to be watching him, and in his mind's eye, the scrolls and inkpots transformed themselves into animated spirits.

Perhaps that foreboding was a sixth sense that only wizards developed—a warning. The more he studied with Zendric, the sharper Kellach's sixth sense became.

He took a deep breath and repeated the secret page spell. The letters shimmered but didn't fade. The writing promptly brightened and returned to normal. He'd lost his concentration again. There was too much noise outside: footsteps, then banging on the ironbound door.

"Who is it?" he shouted. He shut the spellbook and tucked it into the pocket of his robe.

"It's us." Moyra burst in, her tousled red hair bright in the torchlight. "I'm so glad we found you. Where's Zendric?"

Kellach told her, and she shook her head with worry. "Poor Ssarine. I hope she gets well soon."

Driskoll stumbled in a moment later, his sword clattering in the scabbard at his side. Strands of russet hair fell across his forehead. "Kellach. Come at once." He bent forward to catch his breath, hands pressed to his thighs.

Driskoll was shorter, thicker, and more muscular than Kellach, and he wasn't the fastest sprinter in the world. Moyra could outrun him any day.

"What is it?" Kellach asked. "Did you two run all the

way here?" He'd never seen his brother's eyes shine with such excitement.

"You're not going to believe this," Driskoll said. "Even I didn't believe it at first. I mean, how could it be? But it is. It's really true."

"What are you going on about? What's really true?" Kellach glanced from Moyra to Driskoll.

"It's Mom," Driskoll said. "I've found her. She's back."

CHAPTER

2

"Mom? Where is she? What happened?" Kellach hardly dared hope as he locked the door, tucked the spellbook into his pack, and raced after Driskoll and Moyra.

Driskoll yanked open the gate in Zendric's iron fence and ran out into the street. "Come on. She's in Main Square. I saw her at the market."

He tore down the narrow streets in the cool afternoon, followed by Moyra and Kellach. Autumn leaves tumbled along in brushes of orange, gold, and red. The air grew misty with the threat of twilight, when the monsters would emerge.

"How do you know?" Kellach asked. "Where is she now? Why isn't she with you?" His heart sped up. If Jourdain were back, that would be the happiest day of his life. He would tidy his room, clean the whole house, do all his homework. He'd do whatever his father asked.

"We lost her in the crowd," Driskoll said. "But she's here. I know it."

"Maybe you can talk sense into Driskoll," Moyra said as they wove along the dusty streets that led to the market. "I keep telling him that he's hallucinating."

"I am not." Driskoll shot her an angry look as he ran faster. "Moyra and I followed Locky into the market, right into a group of men standing in a circle. I saw a blonde woman sitting in the center, stringing beads—"

"Where's Locky now?" Kellach asked.

"I don't know. He flew away."

"Driskoll!" Kellach fumed. "I told you to take care of him while I was having my lesson!" Kellach had grown terribly attached to the silver, clockwork dragonet—a gift from Ssarine. Lochinvar had imprinted on Kellach and had become the young wizard's familiar.

"It's not my fault," Driskoll said. "He just took off. Anyway, he can take care of himself. He'll be back. He was following the woman—"

"She wasn't the blonde," Moyra said. "I could swear she had *brown* hair."

"You're not making sense," Kellach said.

"Just come and see." Driskoll tugged his arm.

The scents of supper—stews and frying potatoes—drifted through the air, and a wave of excitement washed over Kellach. Their mother used to cook delicious meals, but now, he and Driskoll always made supper before their father got home from a long day as captain of the watch. If Jourdain had returned, the family would eat like royalty again.

"That woman—" Moyra began.

"You mean our mom," Driskoll said.

Moyra glared at Driskoll. "That woman wasn't Jourdain. This woman attracted lots of people, especially men. They stood in a circle with their eyes round and glassy as the moon. Your mom would never have acted like that."

"I'm sure it was her," Driskoll said. "I saw her with my own eyes. I elbowed my way through the crowd, but when I got to the front, she was gone. Locky took off too."

"You should've kept a better rein on him," Kellach said. "Now I'll be worrying until he comes back."

"He'll be fine," Moyra said as they reached Main Square, shadowed by surrounding tall buildings.

Kellach glanced up at the Cathedral of St. Cuthbert of the Cudgel, even taller than Zendric's tower. To Kellach, the circled cross of St. Cuthbert always felt like a benevolent eye watching over him. In the center of the square, the white marble obelisk, which functioned as a sundial, indicated that curfew fast approached.

The merchants were packing up their tents and booths for the evening. By dusk, the streets would grow quiet and tense, holding their breath against the night.

"There's no woman here," Moyra said, standing with her hands on her hips. "I told you. Driskoll was seeing things."

Driskoll glanced frantically around. "I know what I saw." He hurried through the market.

Kellach ran after him, then grabbed Driskoll's arm and forced him to stop. "Look, Moyra's right. The blonde woman was probably someone else."

11

Driskoll shook his head. "Mom was here."

"I know you want her back as much as I do," Kellach said. "But—"

"You have to believe me," Driskoll said. His bottom lip trembled.

"Okay, okay. Pull yourself together. There's no time for blubbering now." Kellach lowered his voice. "We have to stay strong to protect Curston." He didn't mention the image of wings. He didn't want to scare anyone.

Moyra came up behind them, her hands on her hips. "If there's so much danger, why did Zendric leave?"

"Because he trusts us to take care of things," Kellach said. "This is a . . . a test."

Driskoll stood taller and squared his shoulders. "You're right, and we will. Right after we find Mom."

Kellach rolled his eyes. "We'll talk about it later. It's getting late."

Moyra pointed and shouted, "Look! Locky!"

The clockwork dragonet whirred in on delicate wings, his silver scales gleaming, and alighted on Kellach's shoulder. Kellach breathed a sigh of relief. "Locky! I was so worried about you."

"Kel-lach. Not worry," Locky said softly, extending his shimmering neck. Was he holding something in his metal claws? Kellach had trained Locky to scout, not to pick up scrap parchment. But there it was—a folded note clutched in the dragonet's talons.

"Give it to me, Locky," Kellach said gently. Lochinvar

made a strange grating sound.

"Are you broken?" Kellach peered at the little dragon. More grating, not the usual purr and chatter. Something or someone had harmed the little dragon.

"He's injured, not broken," Moyra said. "If you broke your arm or cut your leg, how would you like it if someone called you *broken?*"

"I get your point. Sorry, Locky. Are you injured?"

Locky didn't reply. Kellach pulled at the paper, but the dragonet didn't let go.

"Please drop it," Kellach said.

No response.

Driskoll frowned. "He really is broken—"

"Injured. Come on, Locky. Give us the note," Moyra said.

"I command you to drop the parchment," Kellach said.

Lochinvar clanked and tweeted, then dropped the parchment in Kellach's hand. A faint glow emanated from the paper.

Kellach unfolded the note. A spidery black script leaned across the page, as if blown by an invisible wind. The language was Draconian:

My dearest Kellach and Driskoll,

  How I have missed you. By the gods, I wished every day that you would not forget me. How I longed to return, but events conspired to keep me from you until now.

  I spotted the clockwork dragonet with Driskoll and

Moyra, and I saw my chance to slip you this note. We have much to discuss. Come to the Skinned Cat tonight at the height of the moon—just the three of you. Tell no one else. Come alone and look for me, the woman in the blue cloak.

Yours with all my love,
Mother

CHAPTER

3

"What does it say?" Driskoll, who could not read Draconian, peered over Kellach's shoulder.

Kellach couldn't speak. His throat welled up with emotion. Memories of his mother flooded through him. He felt her cool hand on his forehead when he was ill with fever, saw her throwing a ball to him in the courtyard, and heard her read to him by candlelight, her soft voice lulling him to sleep.

Another part of his mind stepped back. The spidery script could be Jourdain's, but he wasn't sure. The writing didn't match the writing in her old spellbook, but then she'd written in the spellbook when she was just a girl. Handwriting could change over time, and—he had to admit—there *were* similarities, too many to ignore. Perhaps it really was her.

"It's from Mom, isn't it?" Driskoll said. "Isn't it?"

"Yes," Kellach whispered. "It's from her. I think."

Locky let out a strangled wheeze. Kellach petted the little creature's wedge-shaped head. "Don't worry, okay? We'll fix—I mean, *heal* you. But for now, you need to stay in a safe place. Can you make it to Zendric's tower?"

Lochinvar nodded. "Zen-dric. Heal me."

"He's the only one who can. Now off to his tower. Stay there until he returns."

"Kel-lach come?" The dragonet cocked his head.

"Soon, I promise. I have to find out what's going on here."

"Lochinvar—help?"

"Maybe, but you're br—*injured*. I don't want you breaking down altogether."

Lochinvar nodded, then lifted into the air, and flapped away. Kellach watched, a lump of dread in his throat.

"So what do you mean you think the note is from Mom? What does she say?" Driskoll hopped from foot to foot.

Kellach read the note aloud as they headed for home. The merchants from the market spilled past them, all of them hurrying as evening crept across the sky.

"We must go at the height of the moon," Driskoll said.

Kellach frowned. "We shouldn't go out at night. It's too dangerous."

"We have to!" Driskoll said. "Otherwise, we'll miss her. Mom doesn't know it's dangerous for us to go out at night now. She disappeared during the Sundering of the Seal before Curston had a curfew—"

"Besides, since when has a little bit of danger kept you from adventure?" Moyra winked at Kellach, and his face went red.

He recovered quickly. "There's one thing that doesn't make sense. If Mom's back, how did she slip past the watch? All the watchers know she's Dad's wife. Why didn't anyone see her?"

Driskoll shrugged. "She's a wizard. She can make herself invisible."

"But why would she *want* to be invisible? Why not just come straight home?"

"I'm sure she has her reasons," Driskoll said.

"I bet she doesn't want to cause a big fuss," Moyra said. "Maybe someone is after her."

"It's possible." Kellach nodded slowly. In his heart, hope was slowly winning over caution. Mom could be in trouble or on the run from the same evil presence that he'd perceived.

"Should we tell your dad?" Moyra asked as they entered the newest part of the city, the Phoenix Quarter, where the boys lived. At their house, the windows were dark. Torin wasn't home yet.

"Are you cracked?" Driskoll glared at Moyra. "If Dad found out about this, he'd insist we stay home while he went looking for Mom himself. We'd miss out on all the excitement. We can't tell him."

"He's right. The note said we're to go alone," Kellach said in a sober, grown-up voice. "And that is exactly what we'll do."

❙ ❙ ❙ ❙ ❙

Kellach couldn't sleep. He pictured his mother's delicate features—her gentle chin, her porcelain skin, her hair the same shiny, blond shade as his own.

Zendric sometimes commented on the remarkable resemblance between Kellach and Jourdain. Both were tall and slender, with regal noses, the same stubbornness, and the same defiant look in their eyes. Sometimes Kellach caught his father gazing at him with a sad, faraway expression, and Kellach knew that Torin was remembering his wife.

Kellach often wished he didn't look like his mother. He didn't want to be a walking ghost. He lay on his back, hands folded behind his head, and stared out through the window at the bright stars that formed unusual configurations. He identified Ehlonna's Unicorn and Vecna's Eye. His heartbeat quickened.

His mother used to lie next to him and point out the constellations. He'd often wondered if she were lying in bed somewhere, staring up at the same night sky, and thinking of home. The thought had made him angry. If she were enjoying her life somewhere else, it meant she'd left her family behind, and he couldn't understand why a mother could do such a thing.

But he would give her a chance to explain. He didn't want to wait for the moon to rise. He wanted to find his mother now.

He got up, lifted the straw mattress, and felt for a rip in the fabric. He'd used his pocketknife to cut the cloth and hide the spellbook in the mattress three years ago, when a tribe of goblins had invaded the city. After that, he always hid the spellbook in the same place.

He leafed through the pages to the mirror spell. The writing appeared shiny, vibrant, as though it were trying to leap from the page and speak to him. He recited the secret page spell.

Nothing happened.

18

He tried twice more, to no avail. Finally, he tucked the spellbook into the hole and re-made the bed. He wasn't quite sure why he felt the need to hide the book. Perhaps he didn't want his mother to think he'd taken the gift for granted. He got back into bed.

"You awake?" Driskoll sat up in bed, rustling the covers.

"You know I am."

"I can't sleep. Dad snores too loudly. The moon is nearly up. We should go."

"We have to wait for Moyra," Kellach said.

"I hate waiting."

"We promised we'd do it. We're not going without her."

"Do you think Mom will recognize us?" Driskoll asked. "I mean, we've both grown, and you practically have a mustache."

Kellach touched the fuzz on his upper lip. "I wouldn't call it a mustache yet."

"Your voice has changed. It's deeper."

"Yours is changing too. It breaks now and then and gets really high—"

"You're cracked. It does not."

"Anyway, she'll know us. She won't expect us to still be seven and nine years old."

"Remind me about Mom, Kellach. Sometimes I feel like I can't remember her face anymore—"

"She made wonderful dinners—"

"I remember her stews and pastries. My mouth is watering—"

"She had a scent of lavender, and she always read to us before bed."

"I don't know what I'll say to her," Driskoll said. "I know it wasn't her fault for disappearing. She was probably kidnapped, but—"

"Save your breath. We're meeting *someone* at the Skinned Cat. Don't say you know it's Mom. We won't know for sure until we see her."

"I've already seen her!"

Just then, Moyra pushed open the window and scrambled in over the sill. She wore dark clothes and a hood covering her hair.

"You're quiet as a cat." Kellach sprang from bed and grabbed his shoes.

"Stealth is my middle name." Moyra grinned. "Up and at 'em, boys. Ready to go?"

Soon they were dressed and out the window, scaling down the wall to the darkened streets. They entered the shattered, pothole-covered roads of Broken Town. Moyra chose round-about routes through winding, narrow alleyways strewn with garbage and lined with sleeping beggars, the sickly sharp smell of alcohol surrounding them. Kellach wished a different fate had befallen the homeless of Broken Town.

"Keep behind me if you want to stay safe," Moyra said.

Kellach and Driskoll fell into stride behind her.

"And just how do you plan to protect us?" Driskoll asked, squaring his shoulders. He wasn't carrying his sword. The glint of the blade would give them away.

"Experience." She yanked him away from a doorway. "Look out!"

They ducked by just as the door opened. A bottle flew

across the alley and smashed against the opposite wall. Two traveling gnomes burst from the building, fists flying. Dressed in earth tones, each stood about three feet tall and sported short, trimmed beards.

"Traders," Kellach whispered. "They look like twins."

"They're probably brothers," Moyra said. "They're always playing pranks on one another."

"Who got the worst of this one?" Driskoll said as the gnomes stumbled away down the road.

Kellach and Driskoll followed Moyra without another word until they reached the darkest street. Goose bumps raced across Kellach's skin. He could hardly see a foot in front of him. Whenever they came to the Skinned Cat, trouble followed. But he steeled himself as he and Driskoll followed Moyra down to the seedy tavern. The wooden sign squeaked as it swung on its derelict, rusty chain. On the placard, the painting of a hairless panther bared its teeth.

"Gods!" Driskoll said. "I don't want to go through this door."

"We could use the back door," Moyra said.

"That's not what I meant—"

"We don't need a back way just now," Kellach said. "If Mom's here, we won't need to sneak around."

The door swung open, and Kellach pushed Driskoll and Moyra back into the shadows as a couple of brawny half-orcs stumbled outside, bottles in hand. As tall as humans, their scarred skin appeared pale green in the moonlight. Beads of sweat plastered strands of black hair to their sloping foreheads.

They swore in slurred voices as they wove up the alley and around the corner.

"Okay, this is it. Are you ready?" Moyra headed for the door and held it open. She kept the hood over her head. Inside, the crowded tavern reeked of burning meat, ale, and sweat. Nobody seemed to notice the children slink through the shadows. Kellach held Moyra's arm so he wouldn't lose her in the rush, and he sensed Driskoll close behind him. The smoke stung Kellach's eyes. He squinted through the haze.

Moyra turned and motioned Kellach closer. She whispered in his ear, "I have to leave. My parents are here. I don't want them to see me." She pointed.

Off in the corner, Breddo and Royma danced in a warm embrace. A notorious thief, Breddo was always in and out of jail. He was tall, his hair tousled, and Royma's long, copper-colored locks shone now and then in the dim light. As if mesmerized, men were watching her dance.

"What are your parents doing here?" Driskoll whispered.

Moyra shrugged and pulled the hood closer over her face. "My mom never comes to the Skinned Cat. She's always at home working. This is strange. I could swear she was home when I left—"

"Maybe she wanted a break. She can't work all the time." Kellach thought of Royma, her ruddy face sallow and drawn from hours of hard work, her hair straggly and unwashed. That night, her hair looked shiny and brushed, and she swayed to the unearthly music from a harp playing itself in the corner.

"Your mom, look at her," Driskoll said. "All those men are ogling her—"

"Keep your voice down." Moyra put a finger to her lips. She hunched over, glancing from left to right. "I'm not supposed to be here. If they see me, I'm in for it."

Driskoll nodded back toward the door. "Why don't you wait outside? We'll come and get you."

"Are you sure you boys can take care of yourselves?"

"Of course." Irritation scrunched between Kellach's shoulder blades. "I'm a wizard."

Moyra winked. "Okay, Mr. Wizard. Just stay out of trouble. I'll be in the alley." She slipped out the door before Kellach could reply.

He watched Royma and Breddo for a few moments, and the strange sensation of dread whipped through him again. Moyra's parents rarely looked so happy. Men never ogled Royma. These strange events formed a puzzle, and Kellach couldn't put the pieces together.

"Kellach, stop daydreaming," Driskoll said. "Mom's not in this room. We have to search the rest of the tavern."

Kellach nodded, and they wove through the boisterous crowd, then hurried out into the hallway.

"Are you sure she wasn't in the main room?" Kellach asked.

"I wish." Driskoll shook his head. They slipped past two kitchens stinking of meat and broth, a dank privy, and into the network of rooms beyond. From outside, it was impossible to tell that the Skinned Cat sprawled across a few blocks and carved itself into chambers below street level. It was as though the tavern gained a new room every day.

Kellach bit down on growing panic. He focused on looking for the woman in the blue cloak until the words became a mantra in his mind.

Woman in blue cloak, woman in blue cloak. Mom, Mom.

They stopped outside a chamber full of bat-winged beings hanging upside down from the ceiling. A damp, musty smell hovered in the air. "Why would Mom hide this far from the main room?" Kellach mused. "Maybe she's not here at all."

Driskoll pursed his lips. "She's here. I know it." He strode into the room, and Kellach followed, trying not to glance up at the vampiric creatures hanging above his head. A group of gnomes played poker in the corner, the flickering flames from a fireplace lighting their beards. No sign of a woman in a blue cloak.

In the next room, pixies and a group of centaurs danced to the rhythms of ancient drums played by animated drumsticks. Shivers of apprehension went through Kellach. "Look, I'm getting a weird feeling about this. Let's go back."

"No, we can't leave without her." Driskoll slipped into another dim room full of half-orcs playing darts. "We just have a few more rooms to check."

"Something isn't right."

"The only thing that's not right is that we haven't found her yet." Driskoll led down a winding staircase lit by feeble torches in wall sconces. Kellach sighed and followed, but they found no sign of the woman.

Then black wings flapped at the edge of Kellach's vision. The creature—whatever it was—had to be behind him. He whirled around. There was nothing there.

"What is it?" Driskoll asked. "You're pale."

"Nothing. It was nothing. Come on, let's go."

They made their way back to the entrance. Kellach wanted to kick himself. He should have known. Jourdain wasn't there. This was a cruel joke. Who had played it?

In the main room, the music had stopped. A woman with wild, white hair was yelling at Moyra's mother. "You're stealing husbands. That's why you're here, isn't it? Dressed like that, flirting with everyone in sight."

Royma glared. "I'm merely dancing. If you can't keep a rein on your wandering husband, it's not my problem."

The white-haired woman threw a mug of ale. Royma ducked, and the glass smashed against the wall next to a centaur's head. A gnome splashed his ale on the centaur. The centaur stood and upended his chair, then swung a massive fist at the gnome. Men and women tangled in a drunken heap of curses and punches. Glasses flew and shattered against walls.

Kellach grabbed Driskoll's arm, and they picked their way across broken glass to the doorway.

"What do we do now?" Driskoll asked. "Wait here for Mom?"

"She's not here," Kellach said. "We've checked everywhere."

"But—"

Kellach tugged on his brother's arm. "That fight is getting ugly. We should go."

Kellach and Driskoll rushed out into the crisp night air. Moyra stood beneath the swinging tavern sign and pointed down the road with a shaky finger.

There, striding away from them into the night, was the woman in the blue cloak.

CHAPTER

4

K ellach's heart took a grand leap.

Driskoll raced by, nearly knocking him over. "It's her! Come on!"

Moyra emerged from the shadows and followed Driskoll.

"Mom!" Driskoll called. "Stop! It's us!"

"Wait!" Kellach ran after them. The woman in blue quickly diminished in the distance. "We'll never catch up with her on foot."

Driskoll stopped and turned around, breathless. "Do you have a better idea?"

Kellach nodded, closed his eyes, and pulled all his senses into a ball of concentration. He could hear Zendric's voice in his head: *Focus.*

"What are you doing?" Moyra asked.

"Hurry up." Driskoll shifted from foot to foot.

"Just give me a moment." Kellach's eyelashes fluttered. He chanted words he barely remembered from his lessons. He had to get that right, or the woman in blue would be lost to them.

He felt a bit dizzy, and then, in a whirlwind of white dust, a black horse galloped toward them, its hoof beats echoing against the walls.

The creature stopped next to the children, its flank muscles flexing.

Moyra's mouth fell open in an *O*. The steed was unearthly, as large as a young elephant, its mane shining in the dim tavern light.

The horse lowered to its knees.

"Hurry," Kellach said. "Get on."

The trio mounted—Kellach in front, then Moyra, then Driskoll—all three fitting easily on the enormous, magical saddle, and the horse rose to its feet and galloped off through the darkness.

Kellach could feel Moyra clinging to his waist. The wind whipped through his hair, and Kellach couldn't help but smile. The stallion knew to follow the woman in blue, and knew how to navigate the alleys. Kellach felt, for the moment, tremendously powerful.

As they chased the woman, who seemed to move too fast for a mortal, Kellach's limbs ached from the strain of casting the spell, as if the creature beneath him had absorbed all his energy.

Driskoll whooped with excitement as the horse leaped to clear a stone wall.

The horse picked up speed, and suddenly the woman came into view, the cloak flying behind her. They caught up with her at the end of a blind alley.

She halted and turned, pulling the cloak close around her. She didn't seem to be out of breath. Kellach squinted in the semidarkness, the crumbling facades of Broken Town washed in feeble moonlight. He couldn't see her face hidden beneath her hood.

The horse shifted uneasily. Steam rose in great puffs from its nostrils.

Driskoll dismounted first. He stood next to the horse, his hand reaching up to stroke its mane. "Mom?"

The woman didn't answer.

Kellach tamped down dread. Moyra still clung to his waist. "What do we do now?" she whispered.

"Don't worry—I'll handle this," he whispered back, then called out, "We received your note. You asked us to meet you, and then you ran. Why? Who are you? Identify yourself."

"Mom?" Driskoll called out again, his voice full of hope.

The woman stepped closer. She stood bathed in moonlight, but the hood still shadowed her face.

Kellach ignored his pounding heartbeat and the rubbery feeling in his legs. He dismounted and helped Moyra down. She ran her hands across her mussed hair. The horse posted into the mist, its hoof beats fading.

"If you're our mother, explain yourself." Kellach sounded far more confident than he felt. The sense of danger returned, the pressure behind his eyes.

The woman took another step closer.

"Stop," Moyra said in a shaky voice. "We're the Knights of the Silver Dragon, and we demand to know who you are."

Moyra, Kellach, and Driskoll stood in an unfamiliar corner of Broken Town, facing a silent woman who might or might not be Jourdain. Perhaps she is a phantom, Kellach thought, conjured by the strength of our memories.

Then she spoke.

"There, there," she said in a soft, singsong voice. "Who did you expect me to be?"

Driskoll let out a whoop of joy and dashed headlong into her arms.

"Wait, Driskoll," Kellach shouted, but it was too late. The woman and Driskoll embraced.

Moyra hung back, watching.

"You have nothing to fear." The woman's gentle voice carried Kellach upon a calm, tropical sea. He floated in its warmth, and then she pulled off her hood. She shook her head and let her hair loose, its blond, silken strands spilling down past her shoulders.

Moyra gasped. Kellach couldn't move, couldn't speak. It was as if the road reached up and grabbed his legs, rooting him to the spot. He couldn't stop staring at the woman's regal face.

There was no mistaking who she was.

CHAPTER

5

"Mom."

Kellach breathed the word up into the air.

He ran toward Jourdain, all caution abandoned, and embraced her. He, Jourdain, and Driskoll hugged for a long time in silence.

How many hugs would it take to undo five years of separation? A thousand? A million? Kellach didn't care. He would hug her as many times as it took.

He relished his mother's firm arms around him and the lavender scent of her hair. Her smell was familiar and yet new. He couldn't let go for fear she would disappear. He didn't want it to be a dream.

"I thought you were dead," he said. He stood as tall as she did. She seemed smaller, thinner, and more fragile than he remembered.

"I'm not dead, my darling boy."

"I dreamed of you every night for so long. I wondered

what had happened to you."

"I'm here, and I'll never leave again, Kellach," she said in a soothing voice, and the sound of his name brought fresh tears to his eyes.

"After the Sundering, the city was nearly destroyed," Driskoll said. "You disappeared."

"I know, my dearest. I remember it like it was yesterday. Treasure hunters broke the seal in the ruins outside Curston—"

"Curston? Don't you remember?" Kellach asked. "Curston was called Promise then."

"Of course, of course," Jourdain said in a quiet, sad voice. "I have experienced such trauma. My mind is so mixed up. Sometimes I have trouble recalling what is present and what is past."

"You remember that the Sundering unleashed monsters from other realms?" Kellach asked. "The Knights of the Silver Dragon were nearly destroyed?"

Jourdain nodded. "Such a sad fate has befallen my beautiful city. I hardly recognize it."

"Are you hurt? Are you okay?" Driskoll hugged her tighter.

"I'll be fine." She pulled back, staring at one boy, then at the other, her pale blue eyes brimming with tears. "Look at you both. How you've grown. Kellach, you're so tall and . . . elegant. Like a king. Driskoll, you've developed muscles. Hard to believe you're already thirteen!"

"Twelve," Driskoll said.

"Of course, and Moyra, darling." Jourdain let go of the boys and held out her arms.

"Jourdain." Moyra hung back, narrowing her gaze. "Why did you run from us? Kellach had to summon a horse to catch up with you."

"Some crazed woman started a fight. I didn't want to get hurt. Now, come, dear, let me see you. You've grown into such a lovely young woman. Your hair, red as the wild poppies of Lehar. But you still wear rags, my child—"

"My clothes are fine," Moyra said. "Who else knows you're back?"

"No one, my dear. For now, I don't want the people of Curston to know I've returned. The city may be in danger." Jourdain's voice remained soft and patient. Kellach rode the wave of its lullaby and imagined lying in a field of tall grass, the sunshine warming his skin. "I'll explain everything in time."

"I want to know everything *now*." Moyra put her hands on her hips.

"Leave her alone." Driskoll glanced at Moyra over his shoulder. "Our mother is home. This is the most wonderful day of our lives. Can't you just let us enjoy it? She'll tell us everything when she's ready."

Kellach nodded in agreement. He held his mother's hand, warm and firm and real. He would never let go. He knew he looked like a baby—standing there, clinging to his mother. But he had a right. And she knew the city was in danger. He wasn't the only one with intuition. Perhaps he'd inherited his sixth sense from her.

"Be happy for us, Moyra," he said.

"I *am* happy." She wasn't smiling. "But how did you get into the city? How did you slip past the watch? Does Torin know you're back? He's captain of the watch. Surely—"

"So many questions for such a young girl." Jourdain laughed—a wonderful, bell-like ring. "I remained cloaked and wandered in with a group of women. I did not see Torin. I . . . I didn't want to."

Moyra wrinkled her eyebrows. "Why wouldn't you want to see your own husband?"

"Oh, I *long* to see him, but I've been gone so many years. I assume he's taken another wife, and, well . . ." Her voice trailed off. "I don't want to cause trouble."

"He doesn't have another wife," Driskoll burst out. "Not even a girlfriend."

Jourdain's face relaxed. A smile touched her lips. "Ah, then! Let's walk. We have much to discuss."

Moyra turned on her heel. "Follow me. I'll lead you out of Broken Town."

She stayed several steps ahead. Kellach, Jourdain, and Driskoll linked arms and followed, chatting all the way.

At a dim intersection, Jourdain turned to face southeast, toward the distant Wizards' Quarter. "Shouldn't we go this way?"

Driskoll tugged her sleeve. "No, we still live in the Phoenix Quarter to the south. Our house hasn't changed at all! We were lucky. During the Sundering, the entire southern and western ends of Promise nearly burned down. Do you remember?"

Jourdain nodded, and her face softened with sadness.

"I remember—so much fire and noise. Children crying, men shouting—"

"We're rebuilding," Driskoll said. "It looks halfway decent now—"

"No, it doesn't," Kellach said. "It still looks . . . scruffy. The city is under a terrible curse. We shouldn't be out at night."

"I'll protect you," Jourdain said, and once again Kellach felt as though the inside of his head was turning to mush.

"Can you undo the Sundering, Mom?" Driskoll asked with eagerness. "You're a wizard!"

"Could Zendric undo the Sundering?" she asked.

Driskoll's face fell. "I suppose not."

"It will take a lot more than a wizard's expertise to make Curston whole again."

"But your wizardry helped you survive out there, didn't it?" Kellach asked.

She nodded, and then Moyra gestured to them to move into the shadows. They were coming upon the Skinned Cat again. As they passed, they could hear a great ruckus inside.

"They're still fighting in there?" Driskoll looked puzzled.

"They're drunk," Moyra said.

Two centaurs stumbled out the door, their eyes glazed, their manner sluggish. Half human, half horse, they swiped at each other with their long swords, missing each time. They were drunk, or were they? The hair stood up on the back of Kellach's neck. They didn't act drunk so much as drugged, as though someone had turned a switch to slow their movements.

"Centaurs don't hang around humans," Moyra whispered.

"They're trading wine with elves," Driskoll whispered back.

The centaurs ogled Jourdain.

"What are you looking at?" Kellach raised a fist.

"The most beautiful woman I've ever seen," one centaur said in a drone-like voice.

"Hey, she's *my* woman," the other centaur said, and the two resumed their sword clashing.

Jourdain gave them an angelic smile, and they stopped fighting and stared.

"Don't you look at our mom that way!" Driskoll yelled.

Kellach shook his fist. "Get going." Fury blazed through him, an anger he didn't know he possessed. He didn't care that the centaurs stood taller than horses and weighed two thousand pounds each.

The centaurs moved off into the night.

"It's nice to have my boys stand up for me," Jourdain said. "But I can take care of myself."

"Not these days," Driskoll said. "This isn't the same city you left. It's far more dangerous."

Moyra walked in silence until they reached Main Square. "This is where I'll leave you."

"Are you sure you'll be safe walking alone, my child?" Jourdain asked.

"I'm used to finding my way around Curston. I'm a thief," Moyra said, turning back the way they had come. "Or have you forgotten?"

Jourdain glanced down the road. "Now I remember. Forgive

me, child. I've been gone so long. Be safe, and . . . please don't tell your parents of my return. I don't want everyone to know I'm back just yet. I need time to adjust."

"Didn't my parents see you in the Skinned Cat?" Moyra said.

Jourdain shook her head. "They were far too busy dancing together."

Moyra set off at a trot and disappeared in the darkness.

Kellach had the urge to run after her, then changed his mind. He would talk to her later.

He didn't know why she was acting so meanly. Perhaps she was jealous. Perhaps it was because her own mother never treated her as well as Jourdain had treated him and Driskoll. Kellach shrugged. Soon, Moyra would come around.

Although the boys led Jourdain along the safest streets home, Kellach stayed on the alert. But he didn't feel as attentive as usual, perhaps because he'd been up most of the night.

"We're Knights of the Silver Dragon," Driskoll said. "Zendric knighted us and gave us these pins for saving his life. It's a long story." Driskoll pulled the Knights pin from his pocket and showed it to her.

Her eyes shone. "My goodness. I'm so proud of you, my boys."

"We don't flaunt it," Kellach said, giving Driskoll a look. "The other kids envy us sometimes. But we protect the city as best we can. We're supposed to be protecting Curston now. Zendric said—"

"Where is Zendric?" Jourdain asked.

"He had to leave to tend to Ssarine, a medusa," Kellach said. "That's another long story."

"When will he return? I may need his help."

"When Ssarine is better," Kellach said. "You must miss Zendric. He'll be thrilled to know you've returned."

"Yes, I miss him. We won't let him know I'm back just yet, especially with his friend's illness. Does Zendric know when the . . . the medusa will recover? Soon? Many days or a few?"

"We don't know," Kellach said.

Jourdain fell silent as they walked, and Driskoll pointed out the new construction in the Phoenix Quarter as well as the vacant blocks where the burned homes and shops had not yet been rebuilt.

"And there's our house. Remember?" Driskoll stopped and pointed at the two-story dwelling, pale gray in the moonlight, its large, square windows gazing out.

"Home, sweet home." As Jourdain smiled up at the house, Kellach saw something in her eyes, something he couldn't identify at first, and then he realized what it was. Driskoll used to get that look when he passed the candy shop. It was a look of hunger.

CHAPTER

6

Inside, Kellach lit the lamps in the wall sconces. A warm, orange glow unfolded through the front room.

Driskoll dashed upstairs to wake Torin, and Jourdain stood in the middle of the room, taking in the hearth, the tapestries, and the rough-hewn chairs. Kellach wondered if she recognized anything. Torin had taken care to keep as much as he could after the Sundering. He'd saved what hadn't been looted.

Jourdain strode around the room, ran her fingers across the table edge, touched the ceramic bowls and the chairs as if, by handling everything, she could somehow connect herself to home again.

Kellach watched her in silence. How many times had he imagined her there: reading to him, stoking the fire? He'd made do with the ghost of her memory, and now, and now—

"What kind of joke is this? Where were you boys?" Torin's gruff voice floated down the stairs. He'd become a harsh, strict father over the past few years, and Kellach had sometimes wished for his mother's soothing presence.

Now she was there.

"Jourdain?" Torin stood halfway down the stairs, his face white with disbelief. His hair was tousled with sleep, his tunic rumpled. Driskoll hung back in the shadows behind his father.

"Torin," Jourdain breathed. The world stopped as the two gazed at each other.

Kellach held his breath.

"Is it really you?" Torin's voice broke. "Are the gods playing tricks?"

Kellach exhaled and gripped the back of a chair. The world began turning again.

"No, my darling," Jourdain said. "There are no gods playing tricks here."

"Please say you didn't run from us," Torin said. "Say you had no way to return until now. No way to contact us."

"I had no way."

Kellach looked at his dusty shoes. He wondered whether he and Driskoll were meant to hear such talk.

"Are you a dream?" Torin asked.

"It's me. I'm real. Leaving was not my choice. Hear what I have to say." She reached out, and then Torin dashed downstairs, lifting her in his arms, swinging her around and around until she gasped and laughed.

Driskoll rushed down, and then they were all whooping and hugging, giddy with joy.

"We must celebrate," Torin said. "Come and sit by the hearth."

He lit a fire, although it was well past midnight. In a few hours, the pale sun would struggle up over the horizon. What did it matter if none of them got any sleep? They were together again.

Driskoll poured warm cider and cut bread, cheese, and fruit. They all sat by the fire, Torin with his arm around Jourdain's shoulders, stroking her hair. A lump rose in Kellach's throat. He'd rarely seen his father show such tenderness.

Jourdain sipped the cider and shifted closer to Torin. "I have much to tell. But first, my dear boys, you must tell me what you've been doing since I went away. Driskoll, has your archery improved?"

"I never learned to use a bow and arrow," Driskoll said. "I play the lute now—"

"Of course, my master bard!" Jourdain gave Driskoll a warm, approving smile, then turned to face Kellach. "And you, my darling?"

Fuzziness returned to Kellach's mind. He tore his gaze away and focused on Driskoll, whose face bore a dazed expression. Kellach shook his head. If he saw himself in the mirror, he would probably look dazed too. It was late, and much had happened in only a few hours. "I'm a wizard," he said.

"A wizard's apprentice," Driskoll corrected. "He isn't a full wizard yet."

"Same thing." Kellach sat up straight.

"He's doing very well," Torin said. Kellach's ears heated.

Torin rarely praised him. Kellach would cherish the words like gold and tuck them away for safekeeping.

Jourdain's eyebrows rose. She fixed her gaze on Kellach.

"My son. I would never expect less from you."

"I want to be like you. Zendric says you're the best wizard he's ever known."

"He's far too generous, I'm afraid." Her eyes seemed to flicker in the lamplight from blue to black. She laughed—the warm sound gathered everyone in its embrace. "My family has done well."

"So have you," Torin said. "You're looking well. Where have you been?"

As Jourdain sipped cider, she began to talk. "During the Sundering, Zendric and I fought side by side. We battled goblins, renegade giants, and all manner of vile creatures. But when Nahemah attacked me, Zendric and I lost each other, and I lost my family." She gazed at the boys. "I'm so sorry."

"We looked for you everywhere," Driskoll said. "Did you look for us? Did you think of trying to find us again?"

"Indeed, I could think of nothing else."

"She did her best, boys," Torin said.

Kellach stared at him. How could Dad know she'd done her best? He sat pressed against his wife. Torin had never looked so happy.

"Why couldn't you come home until now?" Driskoll asked.

"Nahemah wields a powerful magic," Jourdain said. "I'd battled her before, a long time ago. Zendric and I banished her from the city then, and we never expected—I never expected—she would return. But she did. The day of the Sundering, her powers were too much for me. She carried me out of Curston and took me far, far away from home." The firelight glimmered across her face.

"I knew it. I knew it." Driskoll slapped his knee. "Didn't I tell you she had been kidnapped?"

"Who is Nahemah, Mom?" Kellach leaned forward. "She must be very powerful to have overcome yours and Zendric's magic combined."

Jourdain sighed and nodded. "She is a succubus—"

Kellach and Driskoll gave her a quizzical look.

Jourdain smiled. "Zendric will teach you about the succubi soon enough. She's a kind of monster with green skin."

"A monster?" Kellach shivered. "Does she have wings? Black, bony wings?"

Jourdain's eyes widened in surprise. "How do you know?"

"I've seen her evil coming. I saw the wings in my mind!"

Driskoll gasped. "You did? Why didn't you tell me?"

"I didn't want to scare you—"

"My son." Jourdain touched Kellach's cheek. "A true wizard. Of course you saw her wings. Then you will understand why I was so concerned about making sure no one saw me enter the city. I'm afraid . . . I'm afraid Nahemah may be following me."

"Is she here? In Curston?" Kellach felt a cold breeze on his neck, then it was gone.

"Is she?" Driskoll asked, enthralled.

"She may very well be close," Jourdain said, and she traded knowing looks with Torin. "It may be difficult to tell just how close she is. She knows this city well. Many years ago, she disguised herself as a human and lived in Curston. She was training to become a wizard. Normally, a succubus doesn't gain the powers of a wizard, but Nahemah did. No one suspected a thing, as she was able to mesmerize people with her intense charisma."

"Did she mesmerize you?" Driskoll asked.

Jourdain smiled. "I saw through her act eventually. But she never forgot her grudge. She returned to exact her revenge the day the seal was sundered. She paralyzed me, and her band of golems carried me through the darkest forest of talking trees. The golems were formidable, like none I'd ever seen. Made of stone, they developed immunity to most magic—"

"Not immune to a wizard's magic," Kellach said.

"I could cast no spells," she said.

"What did Nahemah want with you?" Torin asked.

"She is an old enemy, as I told you. Besides, I still have something she wants, something terribly important—"

"What? What does she want from you?" Kellach leaned forward so far he nearly fell off his chair.

"A talisman that will give her greater power. It remains well hidden. I'll never let her find it."

Excitement shone in Driskoll's eyes. "Where's the talisman? Maybe if we find it, we can destroy it and destroy her!"

44

Jourdain shook her head. "I'll never tell you. I can't put you in danger."

"We're already in danger," Kellach said. "Let us help."

Torin held Jourdain close. "My love, we can't let this evil woman find you."

"I'll do my best to keep her away," Jourdain said.

"Tell us the rest of the story!" Driskoll said, slurping cider. "What happened after Nahemah kidnapped you?"

"When the paralysis wore off, Nahemah grilled me with questions and tried to hypnotize me," Jourdain said. "She failed. I did not divulge the location of the talisman."

"How did you get away?" Driskoll asked.

"I regained my powers and escaped. I wandered across desert, mountain, forest, and swamp. All the while, I felt Nahemah tracking me. I saw her wings in my mind, as you did, Kellach."

"Wow, and then what?" Driskoll bit into a piece of thick bread and washed it down with cider.

"Then I grew tired from my journey, let down my guard, and a band of goblins ambushed me. I fought back, drove them off, but I injured my head. I fell unconscious, and when I came to, I was alone, and my memories were gone."

"You forgot everything? Even us?" Driskoll's mouth fell open.

Jourdain nodded sadly, curling her long, slim fingers around Torin's rough, thick ones. "Elves took me in, helped heal my wounds. But they could not heal my memory. For years, time seemed to stand still. I could remember nothing of my past. Then, one day, I was wandering through the woods, and I came upon the lair of a gold dragon. He appeared in the guise of a human. Gold dragons, as you know, are graceful and wise, and they hate any form of injustice. His magic helped me recover my memory, and I found my way home. This is the short version of a very long story."

Kellach gulped his cider, feeling the hot liquid rush down his throat. So that explained things. If his mother had lost her memory, she wouldn't have tried to come home. "And now you fear that Nahemah may have picked up your trail again," he said.

Jourdain nodded and gazed down at her lap. "I didn't want to advertise my return and put the city in jeopardy, but I couldn't stay away from my family a moment longer."

"We'll face Nahemah together," Kellach said. "If it comes to that."

"I won't put my boys in greater peril," she said.

She turned to kiss Torin. The lamps flickered again, and when she pulled back, Torin's eyes seemed darker, shinier. "I can't believe you're alive," he said. "I don't want to be away from you for one second—"

"My love," Jourdain replied, "we have a whole lifetime ahead of us."

The two headed upstairs, hand in hand.

Kellach and Driskoll sat by the fire, watching the flames eat up the logs. Driskoll closed his eyes, and his breathing took on the easy rhythm of sleep.

Kellach stoked the fire and watched the last flame leap and

then die. He would sleep without dreaming of black, bony wings, and tomorrow, the four of them would still be together.

They were whole again. They were a family.

CHAPTER

7

Kellach awoke to the aroma of golden toast frying and the sound of dishes clattering downstairs. Rays of wan sunshine seeped through his bedroom window, reflecting off the dust in the air.

Outside, the city sprang to life. He could hear voices, and footsteps thudded by in the street. In the bright light of morning, all thoughts of black, bony wings dissipated.

He propped himself up on his elbows. Had he overslept? He couldn't remember his dreams. A fuzzy residue lingered in his mind. He was tired. Exhausted. His legs felt leaden, as if he'd run all night. Perhaps all the excitement had drained him.

Driskoll wasn't in bed. His blankets were rumpled, his pillow dented where his head had rested. Animated conversation drifted up from the kitchen. Although it seemed strange to hear a woman's voice in the house, the sound was also comforting. Kellach thought he could listen to his mother's laughter all day. He got up and rushed halfway down the back stairs. There she was, in the flesh, sitting at the kitchen table with Driskoll. He hadn't dreamed her.

"Morning, Mom," he called down.

"Kellach," she replied, smiling. "Get dressed and come for breakfast."

Downstairs, Torin was browning golden toast in a flat pan that stood on short, built-in legs over the hearth. Jourdain sat at the dining table, popping grapes into her mouth, while Driskoll set the table with four dishes and four wooden spoons.

Kellach stared at his father. He'd rarely seen him cook. The square pieces of bread, soaked in beaten egg yolks, sizzled in the pan. The smell made Kellach's mouth water.

"Dad, aren't you going to work?" he asked, sitting at the table next to his mother. She gave him a quick hug.

"He *is* working," she said. She pointed at the pan.

"I'm taking the day off to spend time with your mother," Torin said. "We'll all spend time with her."

"I'd love that," she said. "Torin, my sweet, don't forget to flip the toast." Torin nodded.

"But who will be captain of the watch?" Kellach asked.

"Gwinton will take my place today." Torin sounded too casual for a man charged with protecting the city from intruders.

Kellach frowned but said nothing. Gwinton, a dwarf, was a well-respected member of the watch, but he had no experience as captain.

"You didn't tell me how you found your mother last night," Torin said.

Kellach glanced at Driskoll, whose eyes widened. They

49

were in trouble now, but Kellach chose to tell a version of the truth. "We met her at the Skinned Cat." He braced himself for a lecture.

Torin flipped the toasts. "Is that so?"

"They summoned a riding horse," Jourdain said.

"Yes, Mom was running away. I had no choice." Kellach's shoulders tensed. Would Torin yell at him for flaunting his abilities?

After a silence, Torin said, "It's a good thing you caught up with her. Good thing she's with us now."

Kellach's shoulders relaxed. "So you don't care that we went to the Skinned Cat?"

Torin shrugged. "I'd rather you stayed away from that seedy place. It's not for children."

Teenagers—nearly men—not children, Kellach thought, but he said nothing. He'd rarely seen his father in such an easy-going mood.

"Driskoll, darling, could you bring me a cup of warm cider?" Jourdain batted her lashes, and Driskoll melted in her gaze.

Torin set steaming plates in front of them, and they ate their first meal as a family in five years. They spoke of politics, new construction in the city, their friends, the past. As Kellach took his first bite of golden toast, he noticed that Driskoll and Torin both had dark rings under their eyes, their pale faces drawn, as if they, too, had run the length of Curston in their sleep.

"Kellach, would you bring me more syrup?" Jourdain said. "I'm sorry to be so demanding. I've just had such a time, walking for days. My feet are covered with blisters."

"Of course. You sit." Kellach patted her arm as he got up.

After breakfast, Kellach and Driskoll swept the room and started cleaning the windows at Jourdain's instruction. She sat curled up on the couch while Torin doused the fire. "We're all going to the market today," he announced. "No studies, no work. Just the family all together again. How would you like that?"

"I can't let people see me," Jourdain said. "I don't want them to know—"

"Come on, you can't stay in disguise forever," Torin said. "If Nahemah's around, we'll draw her from hiding."

"At least let me wear the cloak," Jourdain said. "And I shall enjoy a trip to Main Square."

"Sounds good to me!" Kellach's heart lifted. A day with his mother. A day without studying spells! What fun they could have.

"But even with the cloak, someone might recognize my face, and I can't let an old friend see me looking like this." Jourdain touched the faint lines around her eyes. "I've got crow's-feet already. Wrinkles."

Kellach stopped scrubbing the window and looked at her. "I don't see any wrinkles."

"None at all," Driskoll said.

"You're as beautiful as you've ever been." Torin took her hands and helped her to her feet. He wrapped his arm around Jourdain's waist and spun her around.

Driskoll rolled his eyes and whispered, "They're dancing, and there's no music."

"Driskoll, darling, would you do me a big favor before we go out?" Jourdain slipped out of Torin's grip, grabbed her blue cloak, and wrapped it around her shoulders.

"Anything."

"Could you take the mirror off the wall in the corridor?"

"Why?" Driskoll put down the rag and wiped his hands on his tunic.

"You bought that mirror at the market back when the city was still called Promise," Kellach said. "You said you loved the gilt-edged frame."

"I know, my darlings. But my journey has been long and hard. I don't want to look at my crow's-feet. I can't believe how I've aged. I'm not ready to look at myself again. You see, I rarely had a mirror all the years I was away. I did not have to see how my hair had turned gray."

"I don't see a single gray hair," Kellach said. Women were always obsessed with their appearance. Moyra sometimes grew exasperated with her wild, red hair. Kellach combed his hair in the mornings, but after that, he usually forgot about it. Driskoll's russet hair always looked as rumpled as his bedding.

"Just put the mirror in storage. Would you be a dear?" Jourdain smoothed the cloak and pulled the hood up over her head.

"Maybe you should stay home," Driskoll said. "For safety. I should stay with you."

Jourdain shook her head. "No. Your father's right. I can't stop living just to avoid Nahemah. We'll all go together. As a family. We'll buy cinnamon cookies!"

Driskoll broke into a broad smile. "You remember how much we love cinnamon. Come on, Kellach. Help me carry the mirror." He bounded up the stairs, and Kellach followed.

As he and Driskoll lifted the heavy mirror from its hook on the wall, Kellach said, "Don't you think it strange that she doesn't want the mirror?"

Driskoll shrugged. "It'll take some time for her to adjust to being home. To being older."

"Maybe you're right." But the thing was that Jourdain didn't look older. She looked exactly as Kellach remembered her.

They hid the mirror in their closet and went back downstairs. Torin was holding a bag of gold coins. "We'll buy gifts for your mother."

"Oh, Torin, you needn't," Jourdain said. "You should save your money. All I want is my family."

"You've been saving those coins for years," Kellach said.

"It's not every day your mother returns home. We have to celebrate!" Torin said.

Driskoll hooked his arm in his mother's and glared at his brother. "Don't you think Mom deserves it?"

Kellach shrugged and followed his family out the door.

Together, they walked toward Main Square. Torin strolled with a casual air, peering into shop windows. It was hard to remember that only yesterday he'd marched everywhere like a soldier on a mission.

In front of the apothecary's shop, the proprietor sat on the step, smoking a pipe, his eyes glazed and dull. Kellach remembered seeing him at the Skinned Cat. A few minutes later, they passed two dwarves on a stoop, their eyes showing the same dull expression.

Kellach's stomach twisted. He'd seen a similar look in Torin's eyes the night before and had even seen a hint of it in Driskoll's eyes. It was as though a layer of cotton had drifted in front of their faces.

Jourdain's warning about Nahemah echoed in his mind: *She mesmerizes people with her intense charisma.*

Kellach tried to imagine what a succubus might look like. He pictured a monster with green skin and black, bony wings. He shivered and glanced over his shoulder.

What was going on? Was Nahemah following them right now? Kellach considered sending a message to Zendric, but he dismissed the idea. He wanted to show the old wizard that the Knights could defend the city on their own.

Kellach stayed silent, watching the crowd drift through the market in Main Square. But there, the city seemed normal—men and women bustled past him, their eyes bright and normal. Kellach shook his head. Perhaps he was just imagining things.

"This will be perfect." Torin picked up a heavy silver necklace studded with glittering gems.

"Yes, yes, perfect for the lady," the merchant said. He was a sallow-faced man with yellow teeth.

"But it's so expensive," Jourdain said, still wearing the hood. "You'll have to spend all your coins."

Torin was already emptying the purse into the merchant's gnarled hands.

When he'd paid for the necklace, he had only two coins left.

Kellach's throat went dry. "What if we need the money in an emergency?" he said. "Are you sure you should spend all the coins on that one lousy necklace?"

"We'll get by." Torin held up the necklace to the light. "Your mother must have it."

"Torin, Kellach's right," Jourdain said.

"I insist!" Torin said.

"Wise decision!" the merchant said.

Torin fastened the necklace around Jourdain's neck. Kellach had to admit she looked beautiful.

* * * * *

That night, Jourdain tucked the boys into bed. She pulled the curtains across the window, her gaze traveling around the room, assessing every tapestry, every piece of furniture, every crack in the wall. She paid particular attention to the books on the shelves, running her fingers along their spines as she mouthed the titles.

"Read to us the way you used to," Driskoll said.

"What should I read?"

"Read our favorite!" Driskoll propped himself up on his elbows.

"Ah . . . but my boys have so many favorites. Such avid readers, the two of you are." Her fingers hovered over one volume, *The Sorcerer's Apprentice*.

"Come on, Mom. You know which one!" Driskoll lay down again.

Jourdain chose a book with a golden spine, sat on Driskoll's bed, and stroked his forehead. She began in a soft voice that reminded Kellach of lilies drifting on a pond. "Once upon a time, in a kingdom far away—"

"That's not the right story!" Driskoll said, grabbing the book.

Jourdain chuckled. "Don't you remember? When you were just a tiny boy, you loved this story of the prince and the mouse—"

"I don't remember. I never liked the prince and the mouse one!" Driskoll's face reddened.

"Look, we're too old for stories anyway." Kellach yanked the covers up to his chin.

Jourdain stood up. "All right, then. Maybe tomorrow. Sweet dreams, my dear boys." She bent to kiss Kellach's forehead, her lips leaving a tingling trace. Her lavender scent made him drunk with joy, and he fell into a deep sleep.

Hours later, a scraping noise jolted him awake.

He sat upright in the darkness and saw Driskoll's silhouette already sitting up.

"Someone's downstairs," Driskoll whispered.

CHAPTER

8

Driskoll pressed a finger to his lips. He got up, tiptoed over to Kellach's bed, and sat, the mattress squeaking beneath his weight.

"You're making too much noise," Kellach whispered. "Did you hear anyone break in?"

Driskoll shook his head. "The stairs creaked, like someone was going down."

"Who?" Kellach shivered.

Driskoll shrugged. "Maybe it's Mom making a midnight snack?"

Kellach shook his head. "I hear scratching sounds of things moving." He got out of bed and motioned to Driskoll to follow. He opened the door a crack, taking care not to make a sound.

Faint moonlight illuminated the hallway. He slipped out to the head of the staircase. He discerned the outlines of the couch, the tables, the bookshelves, and Jourdain's shape as she pulled each book from the shelf, checked behind it, then replaced the book. She opened and closed drawers, and looked beneath the cushions on the couch.

Kellach's heartbeat raced. He backed up into the bedroom and shut the door. "It's her," he whispered. "She's searching for something."

"Maybe she's sleepwalking," Driskoll whispered.

"No, she knows what she's doing."

"What are you saying? That she's sneaking around?"

"She's up to something."

Driskoll frowned. "She's our mother. She doesn't sneak around. We'll just talk to her." He headed down the stairs.

"Wait!" Kellach whispered, but it was too late. Driskoll was already in the front room. Kellach rushed down after him.

"Boys, what are you doing up?" Jourdain lit a lamp in a wall sconce and gave Driskoll and Kellach a pleasant smile.

"We were going to ask you the same question!" Driskoll took his mother's hand in his. "We thought you were a thief."

Jourdain laughed. "Keep your voices down. We don't want to wake your father. He had a long day yesterday. Where are your slippers? You'll catch cold in your bare feet—"

"What are you doing down here?" Kellach glanced around the room. A few chairs had been moved, but otherwise the furniture was in place.

Jourdain rested her hands on the back of the couch. "I didn't want to alarm you boys, but I've been worrying. I fear Nahemah may be closer than I thought. Did you see the people in a trance yesterday? On our way to Main Square?"

Kellach nodded soberly.

"I'm afraid," Jourdain said, "Nahemah is close."

Kellach scratched his head. "And you thought she might be hiding in the furniture?"

"I was looking for something I left here many years ago, something to help me fight Nahemah."

"The talisman?" Driskoll asked.

"No, the talisman is far from here."

"Then what is it, and why did you have to look for it in the darkness?" Kellach walked around the room, but nothing had changed.

"I didn't want to alarm you, but I suppose I can't keep the truth from you now."

She sat on the couch, the boys in the armchairs across from her. "During the Sundering, I hid a special vellum scroll that holds potent, dangerous charms. I didn't want the spells to fall into enemy hands. Then later, when I lost my memory, I couldn't remember where I'd hidden the scroll. I know it's in the house somewhere. I may need the spells to fight Nahemah—"

"Why didn't you just tell us?" Kellach asked. "We could've helped you look."

"I didn't want to involve you boys—"

"You're our mother," Driskoll said. "We're already involved!"

She leaned forward to touch Driskoll's cheek, and her eyes filled with love. "My boys, I try to keep you from harm's way, and you always follow me in. I certainly appreciate your help, but for now, you'd best be off to bed. It's very late."

Kellach and Driskoll hugged their mother, and then they all tiptoed upstairs to bed.

"What do you suppose is on the scroll?" Driskoll whispered as he got into bed.

"I don't remember her ever mentioning a scroll," Kellach said.

"She wouldn't have told us if she wanted to protect us. Do you think this evil Nahemah is really close by?"

"If she is, we'll fight her," Kellach said, and shivered.

Just then, a knock came on the window.

Kellach looked at Driskoll, and they both mouthed "Moyra." Kellach unlatched the window, and Moyra's quiet form slipped through. Like a cat, she landed on her feet, her hair tied back in a ponytail. "Come with me, quickly," she whispered. "It's my dad. He's in terrible danger."

CHAPTER

9

"What kind of danger? What happened?" Kellach stuffed clothes beneath the covers to mimic his sleeping body.

"I'll tell you on the way. Weird things have been happening." Moyra climbed up on the windowsill.

"Do you *ever* use doorways?" Kellach asked, climbing up after her.

"Not if I can help it." She winked and pulled herself out onto the roof's overhang.

"Should we tell Dad?" Driskoll whispered, leaning out the window.

"No, we don't want to wake him up," Kellach said. "Can't you hear him snoring? Now hurry. Stuff your bed."

"But shouldn't we tell the watch?"

Moyra shook her head. "We can't tell them. I'll explain on the way."

"But—"

Kellach shot Driskoll a warning look. "Just do it."

Driskoll sighed and backed into the room. Kellach and Moyra crouched out on the overhang. The air was cold and filled with the scents of autumn dampness and dirt. Kellach's breath rose in puffs of steam, and he could hear the grunts and groans of distant night creatures coming to life. He clutched the Knights pin in his pocket. He wished Zendric were there, then pushed away the thought. Zendric had trusted the Knights to protect Curston, and wishing would lead nowhere.

Presently Driskoll swung out over the sill, closed the window, then they shimmied down the pipes and trellises to the street. Moyra pattered ahead—a silent, red-headed apparition. Kellach and Driskoll rushed to catch up.

"What's going on? Where are we going?" Driskoll asked.

"Last night, when I got home from the Skinned Cat," Moyra said, still running, "my parents were arguing. Mom demanded to know where my dad had been."

"But they were together, dancing at the tavern," Driskoll said.

Moyra climbed a low brick wall and disappeared on the other side. The boys followed and kept pace.

"That's exactly what my dad said. He said he was at the Skinned Cat dancing with *her* and that she'd never looked so beautiful."

"Either Breddo's cracked or Royma's cracked," Driskoll said as Moyra led them down a narrow alley and out of the Phoenix Quarter. They were heading back toward Broken Town.

"This is really weird." The wheels turned in Kellach's mind.

He remembered watching Royma leave the tavern. Then he'd run outside, but she had disappeared, and then he'd spotted the woman in the blue cloak.

"My mom slapped him in the face," Moyra went on. "She said she had never been at the Skinned Cat. She'd been home all evening. She had no memory of dancing."

"But she *was* dancing. We saw her," Driskoll insisted. "She's the one who's cracked."

Kellach frowned. "Don't be so sure. Maybe we only thought we saw her at the Skinned Cat."

"You're not suggesting that I'm imagining things again, are you?" Driskoll shot Kellach an angry look. "You thought I had imagined our mother, but she's back."

"I'm suggesting that things may not be what they seem," Kellach said.

"Daddy stormed out of the house, and I followed him," Moyra said. "I kept feeling as though someone was following *me*."

Kellach shivered. "I know what you're saying. I keep thinking someone's tracking us." He glanced over his shoulder, but the street was empty.

Moyra stopped and motioned the boys to crouch in the shadows. A group of heavy half-orcs loped by, swinging great axes and arguing in loud voices. Their prominent canine teeth gleamed in the faint moonlight.

When they'd passed, Moyra summoned the boys and broke into a trot again. "I was peeking out from my alcove, watching my parents argue, and Daddy didn't look well. He was breathing heavily. Sweat glistened on his forehead. He had this strange, glassy look in his eyes. Almost as if he'd been hypnotized. It gave me the creeps. He seemed exhausted, irritable, distracted."

"The glassy look," Kellach said. "I've seen it in our Dad's eyes, and in the eyes of others." He was careful not to mention that he'd seen the look in Driskoll's eyes as well.

"Dad's fine," Driskoll said. "He's just happy that Mom is home. You should be happy too."

"I am." Kellach decided to keep his suspicions to himself, for the timebeing.

"I've noticed the look," Moyra said. "Men and women walking around like zombies, not always doing their jobs."

"You're both cracked," Driskoll said.

"That's why I didn't want to alert the watch," Moyra said, ignoring him. "Most of them already have the glassy look."

"We have to get to the bottom of this," Kellach said.

"We're here." Moyra turned a corner, and they came upon Breddo in an alley. He sat slumped on a barrel, muttering to himself. Wine casks were stacked along the wall.

"What's wrong with him?" Driskoll said as they hurried over. "Everyone is cracked. Everyone and their mother."

"I don't know what happened," Moyra said. "I followed him here. After a few minutes, he started muttering and acting strangely. I tried to talk to him, but he just kept on muttering."

Her bottom lip trembled. Kellach realized she was scared.

"Look, we'll take care of him," he said in his most reassuring tone. "We'll figure all this out. Don't worry. Driskoll, help me get him up."

The boys stood on either side of Breddo, draped his arms around their shoulders, and hoisted him to his feet. He still muttered, but he stood up.

Moyra's face relaxed with relief. "We've got to get him home."

"Breddo, can you take a step?" Kellach asked.

Breddo didn't answer, just kept muttering.

"Lift your right foot, then your left," Kellach said.

Moyra's eyes widened. "Someone's coming."

"Shhh." Kellach held his breath. He heard no sound but Breddo's muttering, and then echoing footsteps approached. Much to Kellach's consternation, Moyra's ears were keener than his were, although *he* was the wizard in training.

He and Driskoll moved Breddo back to the barrel. He seemed content to sit there and mumble to himself.

"Hide. Hurry," Moyra whispered.

They dived behind the barrels as a hooded figure turned the corner and strode into the alley. Kellach peered between the casks.

Kellach's stomach twisted. The shape resembled Jourdain in her blue cloak, but how could that be? She was home, or was she?

He couldn't be sure. The hood shadowed her face.

Could the woman be Breddo's wife, Royma? She strode to Breddo, and he looked up at her with joy shining in his eyes. "Oh my love, my most beautiful," he said in a clear voice dripping with longing. "Where have you been? I waited for you."

She did not reply. Instead, she bent down and pressed her

65

face to Breddo's in a long kiss, or what Kellach assumed was a kiss. It was hard to tell with the hood in the way.

The woman stood up and stepped back. Breddo took a deep breath, and then exhaled and slumped against the wall.

CHAPTER

10

The hooded woman turned and strode away. Moyra rushed to her father. His head lolled forward, but, otherwise, he did not react. She grabbed his shoulders and shook him. "Daddy, come on. What did she do to you?"

The boys rushed over, and Kellach yanked Moyra away. "Hey, take it easy."

"Daddy, Daddy. What happened? How could you kiss that woman? Why did you call her your love? What about Mom? What about me?"

Breddo mumbled in reply. Kellach couldn't make out the words.

"What did she do to him?" Driskoll asked. "He's so pale."

Breddo slumped, his breathing labored, but he was alive.

Kellach patted Breddo's cheek. His skin felt warm, almost feverish. "He's under some sort of spell. It's not his fault. Be kind to him, Moyra."

"How can I be kind? Daddy, are you under a spell? Talk to me."

"He's not going to *know* he's in a trance," Kellach said. "He just *is*."

Moyra shook her head, her lips tight. "That woman. She's doing this."

Kellach leaned down and put his ear to Breddo's mouth. He repeated a strange word in a breathless whisper: "Nahemah, Nahemah."

Kellach straightened up. A shiver went through him. "Nahemah? That woman was Nahemah! Moyra? Do you know if your dad encountered any strangers before tonight? Could the woman have lured him here?"

Moyra shook her head.

Kellach shifted from foot to foot. "Look, I have to go after Nahemah." His heart thudded in his chest.

"You can't go alone," Moyra said. "I know Broken Town better than you do. We'll take my dad home and then find her."

"By then it will be too late!" Kellach said. "We have to follow her. Now."

"I can take Breddo home," Driskoll said. "I know the way."

Moyra hesitated but finally nodded. "Be careful."

Breddo stood, and Driskoll helped him walk.

"Meet us back home in an hour," Kellach called out to his brother. And with that, Kellach and Moyra took off into the night.

"She turned right here," Moyra said. She led Kellach up trellises, across rooftops, and down narrow alleys until they caught up with the sound of the woman's peculiar, hollow footsteps. Then from a rooftop, Kellach spotted the hooded cloak heading toward the Skinned Cat.

Moyra glanced at Kellach, the whites of her eyes visible in the moonlight. "Do you want to go in again?"

"We have no choice."

They slipped down to street level and followed the woman. She stood under the swinging tavern sign and stopped. Moyra and Kellach crouched in the shadows.

Then the woman flipped the hood back off her head. Her hair spilled out in dark black curls.

She was the most beautiful creature Kellach had ever seen.

CHAPTER

11

The curly-haired woman glanced to her left and right. Beneath the faint tavern lamp, she appeared to have freckles, a long nose, long eyelashes, and a quirky smile.

Kellach's brain turned to fuzz, and he heard an odd ringing in his ears. He shook his head and focused.

The woman strode into the Skinned Cat, and the door swung shut behind her.

"We have to go in." Kellach ran across the road.

Moyra caught up. "Wait! She may see us. I know another way in. I use it only in dire emergencies."

She led him down the street into a dark alley rank with the fetid stench of garbage. She jumped up and squeezed through a cracked window. Kellach followed and landed in a small, dark room. As his eyes adjusted to the dimness, he discerned bottles and cans lining the shelves. "What is this place?"

"Storage. Sometimes I pop in here to steal food, but only when I'm really hungry." She opened the door and peered into the corridor. The sounds of laughter and music drifted toward them. "All's clear. Come on."

She and Kellach left the room and hurried down the hall. "I think she's in the great room. Do you hear the commotion?"

Kellach nodded, his throat dry. He could hear rhythmic thuds of dancing feet and a chorus singing a sailor's drinking song— something about capturing mermaids in the Pelorian Sea.

They passed chambers filled with all manner of creatures and smells. No matter how often Kellach came to the Skinned Cat, he never remembered his way through the labyrinth of rooms, but Moyra knew this place as though its map were imprinted on the inside of her eyelids.

She pulled Kellach into the great room. Nobody seemed to notice them. Half-orcs, men, and elves packed the place. They clapped, sang, swung their mugs, and danced on the table-tops. Kellach's stomach turned at the familiar tavern stench. He breathed through his mouth. Elbows jostled him, pushing him hard against Moyra. She gave him a wide-eyed look and whispered in his ear. "Look at their faces."

The men all wore glazed expressions. Goose bumps rose on Kellach's skin. Sheep to the slaughter, he thought in grow-ing panic.

There were no women there save one. Through the crowd, he caught glimpses of her.

The curly-haired woman with freckles. In the center of the room, she danced in a slow, hypnotic twirl, swinging her hips. She wore a gauzy, silver dress that shimmered and changed color, depending on the light, from silver to blue to gold.

Kellach couldn't stop staring at her hair, which made him imagine a waterfall, leaves rustling, and the taste of the sweetest cider. He gazed at her bare feet sliding along the floor, moving in complicated, foreign dance steps as the men clapped and sang, urging her on.

All words drained from Kellach's mind. The pounding of feet, the sound of the music—it all blended into an ancient, primal rhythm, pulling him in, lifting his mind onto a blissful cloud.

"Wake up!" a shrill voice screamed in his ear.

He snapped to attention. His temples throbbed, and his eyes felt dry. With great effort, he turned to look at Moyra.

"We have to leave," she said. "She's affecting you too."

"No. We have to stop her," he managed to say. His tongue had swollen and seemed to fill his whole mouth. "All of Curston will fall into a trance."

"Who is she? Why is she here? Why does she want to put everyone under a spell?"

"She's Nahemah. Mom's enemy. She wants power."

Moyra set her jaw. "She won't have power over me or you. Don't look at her."

But the woman's unusual allure drew Kellach's gaze. He conjured an image of Zendric's white beard, piercing eyes and booming voice. *Concentrate.*

"The cloak," Kellach said. "She's not wearing it. Where is it?"

Moyra wove through the crowd, the men barely registering her small, nimble body as she made her way forward. Kellach tried to keep an eye on Moyra, so he wouldn't watch the woman dance and lose Moyra, who was his anchor. Soon she returned with cloth clutched to her chest.

"The cloak!" Kellach said. There it was, folded in her arms.

"She left it draped over a chair."

"You stole it!"

"I come from a family of thieves, remember? That's what I do: Steal."

"Good thinking." They were in big trouble now, but no matter. "The cloak may help us."

The woman still danced. She hadn't yet noticed that her cloak was missing.

"We have to get out of here." Moyra raced for the back entrance.

Kellach stayed right behind her, and then they started running down the hallway. Too late.

The woman shouted. An inhuman screech pierced Kellach's eardrums, as though she were screaming right inside his head. "Stop, thief. Someone stole my cloak. Don't let her get away!"

Kellach and Moyra ran. As they neared the storage room, Kellach glanced over his shoulder. The woman stormed down the hall with an assortment of men in tow.

"Quick." Moyra slipped into the room and squeezed out through the window. Kellach jumped onto the sill, tried to pull himself through, and got stuck. The voices grew louder.

"My robes are caught on something—a nail." He yanked the robes free, then dragged himself over the sill. He jumped down into the street just as the door to the storage room squeaked open.

He and Moyra dashed away, swerving from one dark shadow to another, racing along until he thought his lungs would explode. Footsteps and shouts grew closer. "They're gaining," Kellach gasped, gulping air. His lungs were on fire.

"Follow me." Moyra swung left down a narrow alley. Their footsteps echoed back at them.

In the distance, someone shouted, "This way. I saw them turn left down that alley."

Kellach followed Moyra several blocks down the alley, until they reached a dead end.

A brick wall rose two stories high.

"I thought you knew the way." Kellach spun around, staring at the buildings on either side.

"I must've made a wrong turn."

"A major wrong turn."

"We don't have time to argue!"

"What do we do?" The buildings on either side stood several stories high. There were no windows. Kellach tried a door. Locked. Another, the same. He couldn't pry them open. "Bolted from the inside."

"Then we'll climb." Moyra started to scale the wall, but she slipped back down. "I can't find a good hold."

"Even if you did, there's no time." A tight ball of panic formed in Kellach's gut.

"Then we hide." Moyra headed for a pile of rubble and old bricks.

Kellach shook his head. "They'll find us there."

"We'll double back. Stay in the shadows."

"Are you crazy? They've tracked us this far."

The voices and footsteps grew louder. In a minute, their pursuers would enter the alley. Kellach and Moyra stared at each other.

They were trapped.

CHAPTER

12

C an't you do something?" Moyra clutched the cloak to her chest.

"Shh. I need quiet." Kellach closed his eyes and pictured a giant's front entrance. Silver stardust sparkled across the inside of his eyelids. He opened his eyes and willed the door to burn itself through the brick. —

Nothing happened.

"If you're casting a spell, hurry up." Moyra glanced toward the alley and jumped up and down.

"Give me a minute."

"We have twenty seconds."

The voices closed in, the footsteps only a couple of blocks away.

Kellach pictured a giant green door with a black iron latch. The wall groaned and shifted.

Concentrate.

The bricks moved, swelling and morphing. The footsteps

were only a block away now.

Faster, faster, Kellach thought, then calmed his mind. He heard Zendric's voice: *Patience is one of a wizard's greatest assets.*

"Look!" Moyra's mouth dropped open. "Something's happening."

The wall swirled, and a door formed, giving off smoke and the odor of burning.

"Yes!" Kellach punched the air.

There it was. Too small for a giant, but big enough for him and Moyra to fit through if they ducked.

The gang of pursuers turned the corner into the alley. "There they are. Thieves!" a half-orc shouted in a guttural tone.

"Hurry." Kellach pushed Moyra. "It won't last long."

The wall wavered. Moyra dashed through with Kellach right after her. He slammed the door, his left foot barely free as the door faded and the wood hardened again. Moyra stared at the bricks. Her face paled.

Kellach dusted off his robes and glanced around. They had stumbled into an untamed garden bordered by walls on three sides and a modest stone house on the fourth. One wall had crumbled, opening a path to the street.

"We barged into somebody's backyard," Moyra whispered. On the other side of the wall, their pursuers cursed and swore, pounding the brick.

Kellach grabbed Moyra's arm. "Come on. Let's go."

She stumbled after him. "I have to go home and make sure my dad—"

"Not yet. Not your house. Who knows what's going on there. We said we'd meet Driskoll at home, at my house."

"Wait." Moyra put a finger to her lips. "Listen, they're coming around the block."

The voices faded and shifted direction.

"Come on." Kellach turned left down a narrow alley. Many of the homes here had been destroyed. Piles of rubble stood as monuments to the lives lost during the Sundering. Kellach and Moyra ran through that silent graveyard like ghosts.

When they reached Main Square, they slowed their pace. Moyra walked close to Kellach and kicked a stone. It rolled across the road and clunked into the gutter. "The woman in the alley and at the Skinned Cat didn't look like anyone I know."

Kellach shrugged. "That's because she was Nahemah."

"But she was wearing your mom's cloak. This is your mom's cloak, isn't it?" She held the folded cloak tucked under her arm.

"It looks like it," Kellach said. "Mom probably took the cloak from Nahemah after she kidnapped Mom, and Nahemah got it back—"

"But how?" Moyra asked.

A terrible thought struck Kellach. "Mom was worried Nahemah was following her. Maybe Nahemah attacked Mom and took it back."

"When could she have done that?" Moyra's eyes widened.

"We've been gone a long time." Kellach glanced up at the sky, a cryptic blackness studded with stars. "It must have happened just after we left." Worry rose in Kellach's throat.

He started to run. "Come on, Moyra. We've got to hurry. We have to make sure Mom is okay!"

■ ▮ ▮ ▮ ▮

They slipped in through Kellach's bedroom window and found Driskoll pacing. "Where have you been? I've been home for two hours."

"How's my dad? Is he safe?" Moyra asked.

"Yes. I took him home. The farther we got from the alley, the better he became. He seemed to wake up a bit, but he didn't talk. He was dazed, unaware of me or anything else around him."

Moyra frowned. "I have to go home."

"He's safe, I tell you," Driskoll said. "I took him to your doorstep. Royma answered the door. She'd been awake, wondering where you and Breddo were. You're really going to get it."

Moyra's cheeks reddened. "Then maybe I won't go home."

Kellach turned to Driskoll. "Did you tell her where we found Breddo? What did you say?"

"I didn't tell her about the woman or anything," Driskoll said. "I just said he must've gotten drunk at the Skinned Cat."

"Did she believe you?"

Driskoll shrugged. "Maybe. Hard to say. What happened with you two?"

Kellach quickly explained what had happened, and Moyra unfolded the cloak.

"We think Nahemah stole this from Mom," Kellach said.

"Have you seen her? Is Mom okay?"

Driskoll nooded his head. "She's fine. She's asleep with Dad. They've been home all night."

Moyra sat on Kellach's bed with the cloak draped across her lap. "You know what's so strange? The cloak got heavier and heavier the more I ran with it, until it felt like a great boulder in my arms."

Kellach snatched the cloak and ran his fingers along its satin hem. The fabric still carried the lingering fragrance of lavender. "This is no ordinary cloak."

"What is it? Magic?" Driskoll stroked the hood with his fingers.

Kellach pulled it away from Driskoll's reach. "It's a Cloak of Charisma. It enhances Nahemah's charismatic effect on her . . . victims."

Moyra gasped. "That's why all those men looked like zombies. She cast a spell on them."

"It helped her, but the cloak alone cannot be responsible for what's going on here," Kellach said. "It's merely a tool. The wearer harbors formidable powers of her own, as you saw at the Skinned Cat."

"We have to tell Mom," Driskoll said.

"Not yet—don't wake her," Kellach said. "It can wait until morning."

Driskoll shivered. "Let's go and find Zendric and tell him. He'll help us."

Kellach hesitated, thinking. "He's a considerable distance away."

"We could send Locky," Driskoll said.

"We don't have time to repair him," Kellach said.

"Then we'll go ourselves," Driskoll said.

Moyra glared at Driskoll. "What? Traipse through the dangerous forests and ruins outside Curston just so we can tell Zendric that we need him to come and hold our hands?"

"You're right. We've faced worse than this before," Driskoll said, holding up the Knights pin. The silver dragon glinted in the moonlight.

"Okay. Now we hide the cloak," Kellach said. "But where?"

"In the closet," Driskoll suggested.

"Too easy," Moyra said. "Why not in the drawers with your own clothes?"

"What if the cloak gives off a sort of homing signal?" Driskoll said. "Then she could find it in the drawers."

"No, there's no homing signal," Kellach said. "But if she sees the cloak, she can summon it." Kellach thought of the spellbook hidden in the mattress. He could conceal the cloak there too, but then the bed might feel lumpy. "We should keep the cloak right here, in plain sight."

"What do you mean?" Moyra asked.

Kellach placed the cloak on the bed and imagined transparent cloth, cleansed of color, clear as glass. He whispered the spell under his breath.

"Look, it's glowing," Moyra said.

Kellach focused. Sweat broke out on his upper lip.

Driskoll stared in awe as the molecules of the cloak shimmered like tiny diamonds, then slowly faded. Where the cloak had been, there was only the smooth bedcover.

"Wow." Moyra reached out to touch the empty space, snapped her hand back. "I felt it. The cloak. It's still there."

Driskoll touched the cloak, then stared at his fingers.

As if performing a mime, Kellach lifted the invisible cloak and placed it on top of the bookshelf.

"I have to see if Mom's okay." He put a finger to his lips. "We have to be quiet."

"I'm coming with you," Moyra said.

Without a word, Driskoll flopped back on his bed, hands behind his head.

Kellach and Moyra slipped out into the hall and tiptoed to the master bedroom. The door was open just a crack. From the shadows, Kellach could make out only one shape in the bed—Torin lying on his side, the pillows bunched under his head. At the edge of the bed, sat Jourdain.

Muffled voices came from behind the door. Kellach could hear Jourdain's gentle, coaxing tone. Torin replied in disjointed mumbles. Kellach sidled along the wall closer to the master bedroom. His heartbeat thudded in his ears. Moyra slid along next to him.

He strained to hear the conversation.

"Do you remember where they are?" Jourdain asked.

"Where what are?" Torin replied in a sleepy voice.

"I need the spells. To fight Nahemah." Her voice softened.

"She's back, and I'm no match for her without my special spells. You know, the ones I left behind so many years ago. I must've hidden them well."

"Hidden?" Torin sounded confused. "Please, come back to bed. What are you doing up? It's nearly dawn."

"I can't sleep. I sense Nahemah's presence."

"Go to sleep, darling," Torin mumbled. "We'll work it out in the morning."

"We may not have that much time! I need my spells. I've been desperately trying to remember all night where I'd hidden the scroll, but now I realize it wasn't a scroll at all."

"What do you mean it wasn't a scroll?"

"It was a spellbook. I need to find an old spellbook."

"Oh, yes. You mean Kellach's spellbook."

"Kellach's?"

Goose bumps rose on Kellach's arms. His throat went dry. He thought of the spellbook hidden in the mattress. Moyra tugged his arm, but he stayed put, motioning to her to wait.

"He has it somewhere," Torin said. "He says you left it for him, for safekeeping."

"I shall have to get it from him then."

Torin sighed. "In the morning, Jourdain. The boys need their sleep."

"Of course, my darling." The bed creaked as Jourdain got in next to Torin.

Kellach and Moyra raced back to the boys' room.

Driskoll sat up in bed. "What happened?"

"Mom was talking to Dad," Kellach whispered. "She told him she needs my spellbook."

"Then we should give it to her," Driskoll said.

Kellach shook his head. "I'm not sure . . . I'm not sure she's herself."

Moyra nodded. "Did you hear her voice? It was flat. She's in a trance or something. I think Nahemah cast a spell on her when she stole the cloak."

Driskoll rubbed his eyes. "You're cracked. Nobody could cast a spell on Mom."

"Nahemah did it before," Kellach said, pacing. "Nahemah hypnotized her to try to get her to reveal the location of the amulet, remember?"

Moyra nodded, her eyes bright. "If your Mom's under Nahemah's control, Nahemah may be using her to get to the spellbook. I think this could be a trap."

Kellach stopped and scratched his chin. As usual, Moyra was the voice of reason. "Okay, we'll keep the spellbook hidden in my mattress for now."

"What if she finds it?" Moyra said.

"The spellbook is highly magical," Kellach said. "Much more magical than the cloak is. It's not vulnerable to the same simple spells."

"But your mom's a wizard. She could find it. Shouldn't we take it somewhere safe? Like Zendric's tower?"

Kellach prickled with annoyance, but he knew Moyra was right.

He grabbed the spellbook out of its hiding place and wrapped it in the cloak.

Moyra was already crouched on the windowsill. "Come on, you two."

CHAPTER

13

D awn lit the sky as Kellach, Moyra, and Driskoll raced
through the Phoenix Quarter toward the center of the city.
They passed men, elves, and half-orcs wandering in a zombielike haze. Many merchants in Main Square had fallen asleep
while setting up their booths. Young thieves dashed through the
crowd, snatching oranges, beads, knives, and any other items
they could grab.

"Where is the watch?" Moyra asked, glancing around in
desperation.

"Most of them are wandering." Kellach pointed. A member
of the watch strolled along, eyes glazed, his sword dangling
uselessly at his side. He was oblivious to the shouting and
commotion.

"The kids aren't affected," Moyra said, running after
Kellach. "The adults are all in a stupor."

"What can we do?" Driskoll asked.

"Nothing right now," Kellach said. "We have to get to

Zendric's tower. It's somewhat protected."

Kellach searched in vain for the curly-haired woman with freckles. She could be, anywhere. The hair stood up on the back of his neck, and the air turned cold.

"Maybe we should summon Zendric," Moyra said. "The city is falling apart."

"We'll try to fix Locky and send him," Kellach said.

Driskoll fell back, his feet dragging. Kellach slowed, grabbed his arm, and forced him to run faster.

They reached Zendric's tower, slipped through the gate, and took the tower stairs two at a time to Zendric's study. Kellach shut the door and latched it, then took a deep breath. They were safe inside, for the moment. The room smelled faintly of wax, books, and chemicals. Lining the walls were shelves filled with ancient tomes. Vellum scrolls were stacked on tables, parchments and carpets on the walls, and sculptures and statues crowded the corners. Everburning torches sent long fingers of light across the room.

Lochinvar whirred to life and floated forward, still grinding and grating, then dived and crashed into a chair. Kellach hid the invisible cloak and spellbook behind a row of books on a shelf, then rushed to the dragonet. "Locky! Are you all right?" He gathered Lochinvar in his arms.

"Kel-lach," Lochinvar said in a tinny voice. "Sense of – direction – a bit – confused."

"Your landing was way off-kilter." Kellach put the dragonet on his shoulder. Metallic claws curled gently around the fabric of Kellach's robes. "Loch-in-var is okay," the dragonet said.

"Just stay here for now, okay?"

Lochinvar nodded, extending his silver neck. The scales gleamed in the torchlight.

Moyra strode to the shelves and began checking through the books.

Driskoll sat in Zendric's great armchair and put his feet up on the desk. His face was pale, his eyes dim. "Why don't we just give the spellbook to Mom? Then maybe all this commotion will stop."

"I hardly think so," Moyra said. "If we give her the book, the city is doomed."

"Don't be so dramatic." Driskoll waved an arm. "It's just a spellbook."

"Just?" Kellach shouted. Locky shifted on his shoulder. "It was her most precious possession. It contains all her early spells, in her own handwriting. She went to great pains to make sure only I would discover her spellbook, and nobody else. Don't you remember how I found it? When I was twelve, I was practicing an *enlarge* spell on a ceramic dragon statue. Do you remember? The one Mom gave me for my eighth birthday?"

Driskoll nodded, his eyebrows furrowed. "You kept that statue next to your bed for four years. I thought you were cracked."

Moyra sat on a table and swung her legs. "So what happened?"

"The statue broke," Kellach said. "Can you guess what I found inside?"

Driskoll laughed. "The spellbook is too big to fit inside that statue."

"I found the spellbook in miniature. No bigger than a deck of cards. Mom shrank it and hid it. She must've known that when I progressed to the level of casting spells, the dragon statue would break. She knew I would find the spellbook."

"So what did you do with it?" Moyra asked.

"I took it to Zendric. He restored it to its original size. 'Finally, you've discovered your mother's legacy,' he said. 'During the Sundering, Jourdain hid the spellbook in the statue. She has charged you with protecting it with your life.'"

"Wow," Moyra said. "She knew you would find it and take care of it. Maybe she knew something would happen to her." Moyra picked up a small brass statue of a dragon. It looked nothing like the delicate statue that Kellach had broken. He missed that statue. It had been a reminder of his mother.

"She suffered a head injury, remember?" Driskoll shouted. "She's not in a trance. Maybe she's just not feeling well. You're so hard on her. Both of you."

Moyra glared at Driskoll "We're just trying to work this thing out, which is more than I can say for—"

"Enough. Stop!" Kellach glanced at Driskoll, who sat with his chin against his chest, brooding.

Who could blame him for wanting so desperately to believe his mother could never fall under the spell of evil? She had accidentally brought Nahemah in her wake, and now she was powerless to fight. It was up to the Knights of the Silver Dragon to set things right.

Kellach and Moyra searched the bookshelves and scrolls for information about Nahemah, but they found nothing.

"So what do we do now?" Moyra said. "How do we find Zendric?"

Kellach sighed. He hated having to do this. "Locky, we don't have time to fix you. You have to try to find Zendric. Tell him we need his help at once."

"He's too ill to go," Moyra said. "He needs to be fixed— healed, I mean."

Kellach's heart twisted. He knew the clockwork dragonet might not survive the journey. "We have no choice. There's no time. Will you go, Locky? You don't have to go if you think you're too . . . sick."

The dragonet lifted from Kellach's shoulder and flapped magnificent wings. "Lochinvar will—not—fail you."

"Farewell, Locky, and keep safe," Kellach said.

"Stay out of sight," Moyra said. "Tell Zendric there's an evil woman named Nahemah. Tell him she's putting all the grown-ups—under a spell."

Kellach fought back tears as the dragonet sailed out through the window, his flight path a bit wobbly.

"We have to figure out what to do now." He glanced again at the bookshelves, at the titles crawling along the spines of each volume. Then his gaze lingered on a vellum scroll on the wall.

"What is it?" Moyra asked.

"I know where we can find out more about Nahemah. I've seen the name before. To the Wee Jas Library! We haven't a moment to lose."

CHAPTER

14

Garbage blew across the Wizards' Quarter as Kellach, Driskoll, and Moyra made their way through the deserted streets.

"Nobody's working the bell tower." Moyra pointed up at the cathedral tower, which rose high above the city. "Shouldn't they have rung the morning bells by now?"

Kellach glanced up at the tower. "I didn't hear the curfew bells last night either."

"It's like the whole city has slipped into a trance," Moyra said. "This is terrible."

"We'll fix this," Kellach said. "Come on. Hurry."

Driskoll remained silent, hanging back a few paces.

A block from Main Square, the Wee Jas Library tucked itself into the back rooms of an ancient stone building that had escaped destruction during the Sundering. Dedicated to the goddess of magic, Wee Jas, the small library housed all manner of magical texts, particularly those involving dark magic.

Moyra tugged on the great wooden door. "It's not open. Should we knock?"

Kellach shook his head. "The librarian is probably in a stupor too, and we don't want to attract attention. There's another way in, if I remember correctly." He led the way around the side to a small window and tried the latch. "Locked. Blast it!"

"Back door," Moyra said. "Come on."

Driskoll remained silent, but he followed.

The back door was locked too.

"I could try to levitate us." Kellach glanced up to the windows on the second floor.

Moyra shook her head. "Those windows are probably locked too."

"If you lose your concentration, we'll fall and break our legs," Driskoll said. "And you can levitate only two people at once—"

"Thanks for having so much confidence in me," Kellach said.

"I have a better idea." Moyra pulled a couple of small steel instruments from her pocket and crouched in front of the door. "Stand back and keep watch."

"What are you doing?" Driskoll asked.

"What thieves do. I'm picking the lock." Moyra slid a steel pin into the keyhole, then stuck in another hooked tool.

"Just hurry." Kellach hunched his shoulders against the cold air and shoved his hands into his pockets. Autumn leaves tumbled along the empty alley. Driskoll paced.

Moyra tinkered for a few minutes, then the lock clicked

and the door swung open. "Ta-da." She pocketed her tools and gave a small bow.

"You're amazing," Kellach said.

Moyra grinned.

When they were all inside, Kellach led them through a dim hallway. The sweet smell of stale incense hung in the air. Everburning torches cast a feeble glow, but otherwise the corridor was empty.

They tiptoed past the library and ascended a narrow staircase into the rare book loft—a musty tower with green walls. The floor-to-ceiling shelves were packed with ancient scrolls and tomes. Sunlight leaked through a narrow skylight and lit a desk piled with manuscripts.

The dust stung Kellach's eyes. The sharp odor of mothballs tickled his nose. He detected a faint citrus scent underneath, as if the librarian had peeled an orange.

Driskoll coughed. "What are we doing, Kellach? We'll get caught."

"Then help me. We're looking for a book labeled *Nahemah*. You two start on that side. I'll start on this side."

Driskoll strode to the north wall and perused the shelves. "Are these books in any kind of order?"

Kellach nodded. "They're in alphabetical order by author . . . but I can't remember the author."

Driskoll snorted. "We'll never find it. There are thousands of books in here."

"Just search," Kellach said. "Since when did you become so . . ." His voice trailed off.

"So *what*?" Driskoll narrowed his gaze.

"Argumentative," Kellach said under his breath. "Never mind. Just hurry."

"How do you know it's here?" Moyra pulled out a thick, leather-bound volume. Dust flew, and she sneezed and put the book back.

"I saw the book once, while I was in here picking up a package for Zendric. I tried to touch it, but the librarian yelled at me, said it was off-limits."

Moyra pulled out another book.

"Careful, these volumes are old and fragile," Kellach said. "Some are magic too. They could—"

"Hey, that hurts. Watch what you're doing," a thin, raspy voice shouted.

Moyra gasped and dropped the book. Driskoll spun around.

"And there you go, dropping me on the floor."

Moyra grabbed the book and lifted it, dusting off its cover. "I'm so sorry. I didn't realize you . . . spoke."

The book cover blinked enormous, paper eyes. "Of course I speak. You didn't expect to read me, did you? The written word is boring. I feel pain too."

"You startled me. That's all. I'm sorry. Can I open you?"

The book glanced left at Driskoll, then right at Kellach. "You're not authorized, young lady. I'm top secret. You kids aren't supposed to be in here. You disturbed my hibernation. I was having a perfectly divine dream of being restored and bound in new—"

"We need your help." Kellach took the book from Moyra and glanced into its dark eyes. "We're looking for a book about Nahemah."

"Nahemah. Nahemah. Let me think."

"Think quickly!" Kellach said. "We don't have much time."

"Ah yes. Nahemah. I know the volume of which you speak. However, you are not authorized—"

"Forget the authorization. We have to see the book."

"The survival of Curston depends on it," said Moyra.

"Survival of Curston, eh? The book shifted in Kellach's grip. How do I know your purposes are not nefarious? That you don't plan to set me on fire—"

"Our intentions are good," Kellach said. "I'm a wizard."

The book laughed, its pages shaking. "Wizard. As if that makes you good? Many a wizard uses power for evil."

"Do you know where we can find the book?"

The book sighed. "You children are rather dense. You don't think the girl found me by accident, do you? I knew you were looking for me. So I made myself available."

Kellach stared at the book, its black cover and luminous eyes revealing no printed words. You're the Nahemah book? But the book I remember, the one I saw, had Nahemah written on the cover.

"If you prefer reality, which I consider rather tedious, then you shall have it."

The book's eyes vanished, and the golden words *Nahemah's Story* took their place.

"Shhh—quiet," Driskoll said. "I hear someone coming up the stairs."

Kellach slid the book back onto the shelf just as the door swung open.

CHAPTER

15

A stout man stepped into the room. His bald head shone. Wrinkles mapped a doughy face with a double chin. He wore a long robe cinched at the waist with a black sash.

A cleric.

He tapped a cane on the floor, glanced to the left and right, and stared directly at Kellach through clouded eyes. "Who's there?"

Kellach held his breath. Then man turned his head left, then right. "I am the head librarian here. Who's there? Hello?"

Could he not see what was right in front of him?

He must be blind, Kellach thought, and put a finger to his lips. Driskoll and Moyra froze in place.

The cleric turned left. His cane hit the desk. "Is somebody in here? Speak."

Moyra's eyes widened. The cleric was two steps from her.

What to do? They could dash past the man. They could escape, but they needed *Nahemah's Story.*

Kellach summoned his strength.

"It is I, Torin," he said in his father's deep voice, "captain of the watch."

Moyra's mouth dropped open, and Driskoll stared.

Kellach grinned. Not bad for a novice, he thought.

The cleric turned toward him. "Torin? What are you doing here at this hour?"

"I needed to find you."

"So early?"

Driskoll coughed, and the cleric's head whipped around. "Who's that?"

"I've brought a colleague with me." Kellach glared at Driskoll, who covered his mouth with his hand. "We need your help. The city is in grave danger."

The cleric walked around the desk. "How may I help the captain of the watch?"

Moyra backed up out of the way. The cleric sat in the armchair. Its legs creaked.

"I need to know the story of Nahemah." Kellach's voice, still Torin's, grew scratchy.

"Nahemah." The cleric ran a shaky hand across his bald pate. "I've not heard anyone speak her name in years. Why do you mention such evil?"

"I believe she's returned." How long could he perform the voice alteration spell before his vocal cords gave out?

"Returned?" The cleric leaned forward. "How can it be? What makes you believe this?"

"I've seen her," Kellach said. "And I heard a man mumbling

98

her name." He ignored Driskoll's angry look.

The cleric shook his head. "So this may be why the city has fallen into chaos?"

"I believe so," Kellach said. He wondered whether the man's blindness made him immune to the succubus's charisma. "I've found the book *Nahemah's Story,* but apparently I'm not authorized to read it."

Kellach handed him the book, and the cleric ran his fingers over its cover. "Ah yes. You were meant to find this book, or otherwise you would not have found it."

Kellach frowned. "Tell me what to do. Who is she? How can we stop her?" His voice grew raspier.

"Legend holds that Nahemah passes from town to town, causing chaos. Her name comes from the Medieval Latin *sub cubaire,* which means 'that which lies beneath.'"

Kellach shivered. Moyra's face paled. Driskoll showed no reaction.

"Go on," Kellach said. His throat hurt. He couldn't imitate his father's voice much longer.

"She is a fearsome creature. She drains her victim's life force by drinking his spirit."

"How?"

"Often with a kiss. Sometimes with merely a look or a dance or her presence. Her potency varies, depending on the vulnerability of the victim."

Moyra covered her mouth. Kellach shot her a look.

"How can we stop her?" Kellach asked.

The cleric opened the book. "Speak."

"Finally, I can breathe," the book said.

"Tell us the story of Nahemah," the cleric said.

"You want the long version? We'll be here until the new moon—"

"Give us the short version," Kellach said.

"Nahemah was in Curston, studying to become a wizard. But she began to use her powers for her own evil purposes—to gain power over unwitting souls. When Jourdain, her mentor, discovered Nahemah's evildoings, she summoned the power of the Knights of the Silver Dragon and they cast Nahemah out. The succubus then lost all her powers and abilities to cast spells."

Kellach wondered whether Nahemah's powers had returned, but he dared not ask. His voice would come out a whisper, or worse, he might sound like himself.

"Nahemah is a shapeshifter. And she has rudimentary telepathic powers. If she can see your memory of someone, she can become that person. You will see her the way you want to see her. Nahemah has the natural ability to charm those around her. The closer they are, the more powerful is her charm."

"We've all been resisting her charm," Kellach said. His lips went numb.

"Adults are most susceptible. Most children escape her power."

Moyra threw Kellach a knowing glance. So that was why child thieves ran rampant while the adults wandered in a haze.

"She avoids direct sunlight and mirrors, which magnify and reflect her evil upon herself."

Kellach gasped. He thought of the mirror in his bedroom closet.

Driskoll had been sidling toward the door, and now stood with his hand on the knob.

"Can we stop her with a mirror?" Kellach asked. His voice was changing back to normal.

The cleric glanced in his direction. "Torin, you sound strange. Are you ill?"

Kellach coughed and made his voice thick. "A frog in my throat."

"You should see the apothecary for some throat lozenges," the cleric said.

"Nahemah grows tired of wandering," the book said. "She longs for magic. She can usurp Jourdain's curse, restore her magic, and use people to carry out her evil deeds if she unlocks the Amulet of Power."

"What's the Amulet of Power?" Kellach rasped.

"An ancient, amber stone that confers the absolute power of wickedness upon its owner. The stone has no power for good. Jourdain once guarded the Amulet of Power. She kept it hidden from evil. But now that Nahemah's returned, the amulet is not safe. To save Curston, you must destroy the amulet."

"How are we supposed to do that?" Kellach's voice had become a thready whisper. "Crush it? Throw it into a fire?"

"Once the box that contains the amulet is opened, the amulet will find Nahemah," the book said. "She will attempt to recite the silver spell to undo the curse and become a wizard again. To become all-powerful. There is only one way to destroy the amulet. Nahemah must recite the silver spell . . . and fail."

"What's the silver spell? Some kind of evil incantation?"

"It is neither good nor evil. Its words allow the user to reflect and magnify magic. When used with the amulet, the spell power increases tenfold."

Kellach went cold. "Where *is* the amulet?"

"Only Jourdain knows where it is. But you must not ask her. The answer will reach Nahemah's ears—"

"How will we find the amulet then?" Kellach asked.

"You must search in your own likeness," the book said.

"My own likeness? Why the riddle?"

The cleric tilted his head curiously. "Torin, your voice is most peculiar—"

"I must warn you," the book cut in. "Nahemah, even without her wizardry, can see through several basic spells. She's not easily fooled. And in her natural shape, she can be quite formidable."

"We're leaving," Kellach rasped. He couldn't risk asking any more questions in his own voice.

Driskoll already had the door open. Moyra padded across the room in catlike silence.

"I sense someone else in here." The cleric stood and snapped the book shut. "And Torin, your voice has changed—"

Kellach, Moyra, and Driskoll dashed through the door and down the stairs.

"Wait!" the cleric called after them. They were already

tearing down the hall, out the front door, and down the steps toward Main Square.

They didn't stop running until they'd reached the obelisk at the center of the square.

Kellach stood panting, trying to catch his breath. "If Nahemah finds the amulet, we're doomed."

Moyra smirked. "Not if we find it first."

"How are we supposed to do that?" Driskoll asked. "We don't even know where it is."

Kellach scratched his chin. "But, you know, the silver spell seems familiar. It reminds me of . . . yes! The mirror spell . . . The mirror spell is the silver spell! It's in Mom's spellbook!"

Moyra gasped. "That must be why Nahemah wants your Mom's spellbook. We have to go back to Zendric's—" She ran ahead.

Kellach raced to catch up. "Nahemah knows about the spellbook, and Dad told Mom I have it. But no one but us knows where it is now. I think it's safe."

"I think we should at least check. Come on!"

Driskoll ran a few paces behind. "We should just talk to Mom," Driskoll said. "The book doesn't know everything. It's just a book."

"She's in a trance," Moyra exclaimed. "Kellach and I heard her asking Torin for the spellbook."

"Maybe she wants to keep the silver spell *safe* from Nahemah," Driskoll said.

Moyra snorted in exasperation, "We can't take our chances! If I didn't know better, I'd think you were under a trance too!"

"Leave him be, Moyra," Kellach rasped. "He just doesn't want to believe Mom could be under Nahemah's power."

Moyra sighed and ran faster.

As they reached Zendric's door, Kellach sensed a black cloud drifting toward them, an evil presence descending.

When they stepped inside, the tower was in disarray. The window stood open, and papers blew across the floor. They rushed upstairs to Zendric's study. Books had been yanked from the shelves, and several statues lay in pieces.

"I knew it!" Moyra shouted.

"I don't understand," Driskoll said. "What happened?"

"It was Nahemah," Kellach said. "She must've been following us."

He reached behind the books. The cloak and the spellbook were gone.

CHAPTER

16

"W hat will we do now?" Moyra said. She gathered scrolls and put them back on the desk.

Kellach picked up books and returned them to the shelves. "Just give me a moment to think."

"We should go home," Driskoll said. His eyes were dark and glazed. "Mom can help us. She'll know what to do." He refused to help straighten the room. Instead, he started marching toward the door. "Let's go get her."

Moyra glared at Kellach. "I told you! He's in a trance, just like your mom!"

"But the book said most children couldn't be affected by Nahemah."

"Maybe he's one of the few exceptions. Maybe he's fallen under Nahemah's spell because he so desperately wants to believe your mother has brought good in her wake."

Kellach glanced at Moyra and sighed. He remembered how he had felt that night at the Skinned Cat, back when he still believed everything was going to be all right. He, too, had felt the power of Nahemah's spell.

He couldn't deny it any longer. Moyra was right.

He rested his hands on Driskoll's shoulders and looked his brother in the eyes. "Driskoll. Listen to me. In the Skinned Cat, Nahemah's charisma put everyone in a weird trance. Even my brain got fuzzy. We think you might have been affected too."

"I'm not in a trance." Driskoll stepped back and stood tall and defiant.

"Nahemah's powers work even from a distance. I think you may be under her spell."

"I'm fine!" Driskoll said.

Kellach and Moyra glanced at each other. "Driskoll, you don't have to help us," Kellach said in a firm voice. "But I want you to stay with us."

"Where would I go?"

To Mom. And if Mom told Nahemah, and Nahemah found the amulet and correctly recited the spell, Nahemah would gain the power to do *more* than simply put Driskoll in a trance. She would *use* him for her wicked purposes. She would use everyone.

Kellach tamped down fear and feigned nonchalance. "We can't lose each other in all this chaos, and you'll be a great help if we have to battle monsters, Driskoll."

"Oh, yeah?" Driskoll puffed up with pride. "I *am* getting stronger."

"You're very strong," Moyra said. She gave Driskoll a sweet smile, but her eyes were sad.

"So you noticed." Driskoll grinned.

Kellach stared at him and for the first time wasn't sure he felt safe in Driskoll's company.

Kellach remembered pretend-fencing with Driskoll when both boys were little; playing ball in the courtyard; sharing each other's allowance; trading sweets; talking in bed until the wee hours of the morning. Kellach had fought the bullies before Driskoll had grown sturdy enough to defend himself.

Together, the brothers had saved Zendric's life, had fought enemies, and had mourned the loss of their mother. Driskoll was more than a brother. He was Kellach's best friend, and now Driskoll wasn't himself, and Kellach had to save him.

Just then, Lochinvar whirred and clanked in through the window, hit the desk, and toppled on his side. Scraping and grating sounds rose from his innards.

"Locky, what happened? Are you all right?" Kellach knelt and righted the dragonet. "Did you find Zendric?"

Lochinvar spluttered and coughed, then spoke in Draconian.

"He says he was ambushed," Kellach translated. "He needs repair."

"Was he ambushed on his way to find Zendric?" Moyra asked. "Or on the way back?"

The dragonet tweeted again.

"On the way to Zendric. He never got there. He would've been destroyed. He's none too comfortable now."

Kellach stood and pressed the palm of his hand to his own forehead.

"How far did he get?" Moyra paced, tapping her finger against her teeth.

More tweets and scraping.

"Halfway to Medusa Island."

"Only halfway?"

Kellach nodded and sat heavily on a chair. His shoulders slumped. His limbs grew heavy. "Great, just great. Why does everything have to go wrong?"

Moyra came to him and put her hands on his shoulders. "You can't give up," she whispered, and nodded toward Driskoll, who was reading a book. "Curston depends on us, depends on you."

Kellach sighed. "We have to find Zendric. I have no idea how—"

"We don't have time, and we don't need Zendric. Come on. We've got to find the amulet. We can do it."

"How?"

"The book said you'd have to look in your own likeness." Moyra paused for a moment in thought. "What do you think that means?"

Kellach shrugged. "I don't know."

Moyra slugged his shoulder. "Come on, Kellach. You're supposed to be the brainy one. Think!"

For a moment, they were both silent. Moyra stared at one of the tapestries hanging on the walls. She snapped her fingers. "I've got it! Your own likeness must be a picture of you! Did your parents ever have any portraits painted of you?"

"I don't think so . . . " Kellach said.

"Let's go look! Maybe they just didn't tell you!" She was already at the door.

Kellach got up and followed, although his heart still felt heavy.

"Come on, Driskoll," he said. "Locky, wait here and lie low."

The dragonet nodded and wrapped magnificent wings around its silver body.

Driskoll put down the book and followed. It took them twice as long as usual to get home. Stores had been looted, and their proprietors loitered in the streets.

At home, there was no sign of Torin.

"Mom, we're home!" Driskoll called, racing upstairs. There was a long pause, then, "Kellach! Moyra! Come here. Quick!"

CHAPTER

17

ellach and Moyra dashed upstairs after him. They found Driskoll standing over Jourdain, who lay in bed, staring at the ceiling.

Kellach took her by the shoulders and gently shook her. "Mom, are you all right? Mom!"

"Kellach—," she whispered. Her pupils were dilated, her skin pale and cool.

"No, Mom. Fight Nahemah." Kellach hugged her. She went limp in his arms.

"What's wrong with her?" Driskoll asked, his voice flat.

"She's under Nahemah's spell, just like you," Moyra said.

Kellach stroked his mother's hair. "Don't give up, Mom. We'll find the amulet. We'll help you."

He let his mother lie down again and adjusted the pillow under her head. Her chest rose and fell in an even rhythm, as if she slept. He held her cool hand in his. "Mom, can you tell us anything to help us fight Nahemah?"

Her eyes cleared and turned blue again for a moment. Her grip tightened on Kellach's hand. "The . . . amulet," she whispered. "Must . . . bring it to me. Fight . . . Nahemah." Then her eyes turned black and vacant again.

"Mom!" Kellach said.

"Do something," Moyra said. "Can't you try a spell to break the trance?"

"There's nothing I can do." Kellach's body felt numb.

"Come on then. Don't just stand there." Moyra tugged his arm. "We've got to find a picture of you."

Kellach tore himself away reluctantly. "You search downstairs, and I'll search the bedrooms." He trudged to his room as Moyra headed downstairs.

Driskoll followed Kellach. "What do you hope to accomplish?"

Kellach's rib cage tightened. He searched beneath the beds in his room and through the books on the nightstand shelf. Nothing.

"Don't you wonder why Mom's lying in bed like that, Driskoll? Don't you wonder why she didn't want anyone to know she was home? She's worried about Nahemah following her."

"She wanted time alone with her family," Driskoll said.

Kellach sighed. He had to stop trying to explain. Reason held little power over evil. He checked the tapestries and all the paintings on the walls.

Driskoll sat on his bed, his brows furrowed. "You're both cracked," he said in a faint voice.

Kellach glanced out the window. The street was empty, but

the black wings flapped across his mind again. Nahemah was moving closer.

He ran to the head of the stairs. "Any luck, Moyra?"

She was searching the shelves, leafing through every book. "No portraits here," she said finally. "We don't have time to check every nook and cranny. Think. Where would your parents keep a picture of your likeness?"

A narrow sunbeam slanted in through the hallway window. Dust particles swirled in the light.

Kellach gripped the banister, his eyes fixed on the beam of light. "Sunlight," he breathed.

"Sunlight? What does that have to do with anything?"

Kellach's eyes snapped back to Moyra. "I just remembered something the book said. Nahemah avoids direct sunlight and mirrors, which magnify and reflect her evil upon herself. The book said I'd have to search in my own likeness. A picture isn't the only likeness of myself. My own likeness could be a reflection. That's it!" Kellach pumped his arm in the air.

"I don't get it." Moyra said.

Kellach raced back up the stairs. "You don't have to. I know where to find the amulet. Hurry."

CHAPTER

18

D riskoll sat up as Kellach and Moyra entered his room. "What are you doing?"

"Don't worry about anything." Kellach opened the closet. "Moyra and I have this under control."

Driskoll lay back on his bed and stared at the ceiling, his eyes black and vacant.

Kellach's heart squeezed, but he got down to business. "Moyra, help me get the mirror out of here."

She helped Kellach haul the heavy mirror out of the closet and prop it against the wall.

"Mom made us remove it when she got home," Kellach whispered. He glanced at Driskoll, who didn't seem to be listening. "She said she didn't want to see how old she'd become." Kellach ran his fingers along the edge of the mirror, looking for a clue. "She lied. She had us hide the mirror because she was preparing the house for Nahemah's arrival."

"That's too scary, Kellach." Moyra's hands trembled. "She

must have been under Nahemah's power from the day we found her."

Kellach nodded.

Driskoll sighed, tucking his hands behind his head. "There's nothing wrong with Mom, and there's no Nahemah."

Kellach tried to ignore Driskoll, but he was getting worse. "The amulet must be hidden in the mirror—move back. I'll try a spell."

He raised his arms and chanted a simple reveal spell. "O mirror, holder of our likeness, spill forth your secrets."

"Spill forth?" Moyra laughed.

"Quiet!" Kellach's cheeks heated. He waved his arms and continued. *"Dissignare, distillare . . . "* He commanded the mirror to open and expose its contents. Nothing happened. His face, brows furrowed in consternation, gazed back at him.

"Just let me try," Moyra said.

"You don't know the spells. Just wait. I'll try another one." He concentrated. *"O, obgrunnire mystax!"*

The mirror didn't change.

"Are you sure 'mystax' is the right word?" Moyra asked. "That sounds like 'mustache.'"

"I know what I'm doing," Kellach snapped. He tried another spell. *"Disclausus!* Open! Disclose your secret!"

Nothing.

"Step aside!" Moyra said, pushing her way forward. "This is ridiculous. There's a simple solution. I bet there's a space between the wood and the mirror." She kneeled and managed to pry away the wooden backing.

Kellach watched, the heat traveling to his ears.

A flat, worn, folded piece of vellum fell from the mirror. "Look, what did I tell you?" Moyra pointed in triumph.

"It's not the amulet," Driskoll said, sitting up in bed.

Kellach hands shook as he unfolded the parchment, written in the ink of an ancient hand. "No," he said. "It's a map."

CHAPTER

19

Kellach tried to decipher the complicated drawings and arrows. "There. That looks like the outskirts of Curston to the south."

Moyra traced the thick, black line with her finger. "These are tunnels—"

"Underground tunnels," Kellach said, still keeping his voice low. "And there. That X. That must be where we'll find the . . . you know what."

Driskoll hummed to himself.

Kellach focused on the map. "We have to go. We'll need supplies."

"What if Nahemah follows us?" Moyra whispered.

"We'll just have to hurry. I sense her."

Moyra's eyebrows lifted. "Sense her?"

"I've come to be able to know when she's around. She's like an . . . evil presence."

"Wait, look." Moyra pointed to the lower left corner of the

map. "There's a bunch of writing here in miniature. Can you read it?"

Kellach rummaged on his shelves for a magnifying glass. "It's written in Draconian. Specifies what we're to take with us."

"What if this is a trap? I mean, why wouldn't your mom have told you about the map when you were younger?"

"She hoped we'd never have to use it," Kellach said solemnly.

"But now Nahemah is back—"

"And we haven't a moment to lose. Here, look." He read the inscription aloud.

Kellach: If Nahemah returns, and I am incapacitated, you must retrieve the amulet. To ensure your safety, carry meat wrapped in cloth, a vial of perfume, chalk, a lamp, and a small palette of oil paints. Good luck, my darling.

Moyra tapped her teeth again. "Now I know it's a trap. A small palette of oil paints? Are we going to become artists or find the amulet? Why do we need chalk? Where will we find perfume? This is cracked."

"I think my mom keeps some scented oil in her hope chest. The one at the foot of her bed," Kellach said.

Moyra looked doubtful.

"Come on, help me put the mirror back in the closet and gather the supplies," Kellach said. "We have to trust the map."

"Trust a piece of old, yellowed parchment?" Moyra frowned and sighed. "Okay, if it helps us find the amulet."

She and Kellach rushed around, returning the mirror to its hiding place, then gathering matches, chalk, a small lamp, and a wooden box filled with oil paints. Moyra found a smoked ham in the pantry. Upstairs, in his parents' room, Kellach opened his mother's old cedar chest.

He picked through her treasures until he found the vial he was looking for. He read the faded label on its base.

"Perfect," he whispered. He shoved the vial into his pack then went back to check on Driskoll.

His brother lay half-asleep on his bed.

Moyra was standing over him. She touched his forehead. "He's warm. Do you suppose we should take him to Latislav?"

Kellach shook his head. "Latislav is probably under Nahemah's spell. I'm feeling a bit sluggish too, as though I could lie down and sleep. And I have a terrible urge to find Nahemah and give her the map, but I'm still myself. I won't give in to the temptation."

"What makes us immune? Why are we still in control?"

"The book said Nahemah usually doesn't affect children. Zendric's teachings have helped me too. I practice concentration and resistance. It's like hypnosis. Some people are more vulnerable than others."

"What shall we do with Driskoll? Look at him."

Kellach snapped his fingers in front of Driskoll's face. No response.

"We can't take him with us," Moyra said. "He'll slow us down."

Kellach snapped again. "Just let me find out if he wants to come with us to help. Maybe we can still—"

"He can hardly move, let alone run. Who knows what we'll find in the caves?"

Kellach sighed. "Maybe he can help us. Maybe he knows something we don't know. Driskoll. Wake up."

Driskoll's eyes fluttered open. He gave them a feeble smile.

"Driskoll, we're going to find the amulet," Kellach said. "Are you coming with us?"

"Is Mom going?" Driskoll's eyes were black pools of nothingness.

Kellach's stomach twisted. "No, Mom is not going. We're going alone, and we'll be facing terrible danger."

"Danger." Driskoll's gaze drifted up to the ceiling. "Mom saves us from danger."

Moyra shook her head slowly. She covered Driskoll with extra blankets. He closed his eyes. Soon his breathing became deep and regular.

"He's asleep," Kellach said. "Let's go."

CHAPTER

20

Kellach and Moyra slipped through the Phoenix Quarter and headed toward the Oldgate. Kellach tried not to focus on the vacant eyes of people he knew as friends. Mere shells now, their bodies wandered beneath Nahemah's spell.

Kellach felt an increased sense of responsibility, but for once, he didn't feel important. He felt terribly small and insignificant under the weight of evil. But he had to fight for Moyra, for Driskoll, for his mother, for everyone he knew and loved.

"The city is falling apart." Moyra whispered, sticking close to Kellach. She kicked a pile of banana peels and garbage off the road.

"We won't let it," Kellach replied. "Just ignore it. Come on."

"How can I? Look at the dogs. Mangy. They're hungry. The children—"

"Ignore them. We can't do any good here. Focus on our mission."

"Our mission." Her voice wavered, but she kept pace. The refuse collectors weren't working. The shopkeepers ambled listlessly, the doors of their shops squeaking open in the wind. A fine film of dust settled over the streets.

The odors of rot and neglect hung in the air. Near the Oldgate, a group of half-orcs milled about, bumping into each other. Kellach and Moyra shouldered their way through the zombielike throng and slipped through the gate.

"There are no watchers," Moyra said, pointing up to the lookout towers. Kellach glanced up. The lookout posts stood dark and empty. Come nightfall, the monsters would descend on the city and rip it to shreds, and nobody would resist.

"Come on, don't look back," he said, pressing forward. Moyra nodded, pulling her tattered hood up over her head. She was one plucky girl. Kellach had to give her that. They were leaving behind Torin, Breddo, her mother, Driskoll—everyone. Leaving them behind for Nahemah. But they had no choice, and they both knew it.

Outside the gate, Curston gave way to hills and valleys dotted with groves of oak, cypress, and elm trees.

Dandelions sprang up here and there, and a mouse scuttled across the path.

Moyra picked a dandelion and tucked it into her pocket. "For safekeeping," she said.

Kellach forced a smile. The calm countryside was deceptive. He sensed vile creatures moving about in the shadows. Monsters pounced on any opportunity to attack Curston residents who wandered too far from home.

Moyra walked stiffly beside Kellach. She acted bravely, yet Kellach knew she was a little scared. But with danger came freedom. They were out, and they were still alive. For the moment.

A bloodcurdling scream echoed down through the valley, borne on the breeze. Moyra stopped. "Maybe this wasn't such a good idea. Maybe we should fight Nahemah face to face."

"No. My mom knew what she was doing when she hid the map. She knew that, someday, we would find it. She knew we would rise to the challenge."

"All I want to do is rise for breakfast and see my dad the way he was before," Moyra said mournfully.

"You will. You're stronger than you know, Moyra. So am I. Zendric knew it. He knows it now. I can't help but believe he would return if we really needed him. He trusts us." Kellach squeezed her shoulder and gazed into her eyes. He tried to give her his inner strength, but then he saw that she didn't need it. Her eyes reflected renewed determination.

She let out a great sigh. "So, which way do we go?"

He consulted the map, then pointed in the direction of the scream.

"Of course. I should've known." Moyra grinned, back to her old self. Squaring her shoulders, she led the way.

They hiked through shaded copses and fields of wild roses. Robins and chickadees twittered and scolded, flitting about in the trees.

Kellach had traversed these trails with his mother and had watched her pick flowers and herbs. He'd discussed philosophy with her and wizardry. She'd never treated him as if he were too young or too stupid to learn.

Now she lay in a trance, her powers dampened by Nahemah's evil. He missed her with a sharp pang in his chest.

"Do you smell that?" Moyra twitched her nose.

"The roses?"

"No, something else. Something underneath."

Kellach walked a few more paces. "Now I smell it too." The stink of sweat, as if a thousand men hadn't washed themselves in years, now approached from the thickening forest ahead.

"What is it?" Moyra held her nose.

"I don't know." In fact, Kellach did have an idea. But he didn't want to alarm Moyra. She was already jumpy.

She glanced at him. "Monsters in that forest, right?"

"I think so."

"Big ones, right?"

He nodded. His throat went dry.

"We don't have weapons," Moyra said.

"Where's Driskoll when we need him?" His laugh sounded forced. "We could use his sword."

"We have your spells," Moyra whispered. "And my stealth and brains."

Kellach glanced at the steep, shale hills to the right and left of the forest. "We can't go around," he said. "And who's to say there aren't monsters in the hills?"

"Then we go through."

"Through?" The stench grew stronger in the forest, and

Kellach's stomach heaved. But he wouldn't vomit. He had to stay focused.

Moyra held her nose and breathed through her mouth, and then the first rock hit. The size of a fist, the granite sailed through the trees and landed a few inches from Moyra's feet. Then another rock ricocheted off a nearby oak. Then another landed with a hollow *thunk* in the trail. Then more rocks, hurled from a distance. One hit Kellach's shin. Pain raced up his leg.

"Run!" he shouted. He and Moyra burst into a sprint, dodging the clumsily thrown rocks. Luckily, whoever was hurling them had terrible aim. The ground shuddered. Immense thuds shook the forest floor behind them. The mottled leaves trembled, some falling to the ground.

Moyra ran faster, throwing Kellach a wide-eyed look. "What's that noise? What's chasing us?"

Kellach risked glancing over his shoulder, his suspicions confirmed. "Athachs. A gang of four or five males," he said. "Run faster."

"I can't."

"They're carrying clubs."

"Great."

"We can't outrun them."

"We could climb a tree," Moyra said.

"They'll tear down the tree in an instant."

"We're dead."

"Not so fast. Let me think."

"No time for thinking, Kellach. We're no match for them. They're too big."

She was right.

Greenish, hulking giants, the athachs rose as tall as the trees and each had three heavily muscled arms, with one growing directly out of their chests. Shabby rags and furs flapped on their backs as they lumbered along on bulbous feet. Curving tusks jutted upward from their lower jaws, and stolen, glittering jewels glinted on their wrists and fingers. Kellach knew their tiny eyes could barely make out shapes at a distance, which explained their terrible aim. They moved in an awkward shamble, but their height gave them speed.

"Kellach," Moyra panted, "you have to do something."

"Give me a minute—"

"Do it. Now!"

Kellach focused his mind and energy into weaving a cloak of concealment around him and Moyra. The air swirled into a cloud, enveloping them in a misty shroud.

He yanked her off the trail. They crouched behind an oak tree as the shroud hardened into a protective, transparent wall. Although Kellach and Moyra could see through the wall, the athachs could not. They would look right through Kellach and Moyra and see only the forest.

At least, Kellach hoped so.

A rabbit bumped into Kellach's leg and then bounded off, dazed, into the undergrowth. The spell had worked! But would the athachs fall for it as well?

The athachs caught up, their tiny noses sniffing the air. Kellach's heart pounded so loudly he thought the athachs would hear it.

Moyra stiffened, eyes wide. The athachs muttered at one another in guttural growls. Slobber dripped from their lips. Close up, the gems glittered on their immense fingers.

Please, please don't see us, Kellach thought. Walk on. Forget about us.

The athachs stepped so close that their breath heated Kellach's head. Slobber dripped on his hair and dribbled onto his cheek, but he dared not wipe off the sticky moisture. He could see the athachs' coarse skin, and their grunts reverberated in his ears. An eternity passed, and then the creatures lumbered down the trail, still conversing in their rough language. Then they abruptly turned, all gazing toward Kellach and Moyra.

"They know we're here," she whispered.

"Wait. Don't move. They don't see us."

"They do. They're coming back."

The athachs retraced their steps, massive brows furrowed. Think, think, Kellach told himself. Focus.

Athachs loved gems and crystals. They were known to sit for hours, polishing and admiring their jewels. But what else did they love above all else? There was something else.

Food.

"The ham," Kellach said. That's why the map instructions included meat.

Moyra was already rummaging in the pack. Her nimble, pick-pocket fingers grabbed the smoked ham in a trice. She threw it to Kellach, and he heaved a small piece into the path. The athachs gathered around the meat, slobbering and fighting over it. Then he tossed another, farther this time, and the athachs moved off.

"Here, let me." Moyra grabbed the entire ham and hurled it a great distance.

Kellach blinked at her. "How did you—"

"While you're learning wizardly spells, I'm out using my arms." She squeezed her fist to show off a firm biceps.

"I'm strong too. I could've thrown it."

"I couldn't take a chance." Moyra winked at him, and he frowned, but this wasn't a time to argue about who was stronger. The athachs rumbled away, drawn by their craving for food.

Kellach and Moyra dashed down the trail, running in desperate silence until the forest thinned, and then they kept running and running until their lungs gave out and they both staggered to a halt, tumbling to the ground and gasping for air.

"We made it." Moyra laughed. "We escaped them, didn't we?"

"Those silly athachs. Their stomachs rule them." Kellach grinned. "We did it, partner." He and Moyra shook hands, reveling in their narrow escape. They were both dirty and covered in sweat. Then they sobered and gazed ahead. In the distance, the trail ended at the dark mouth of a cave built into the hillside.

Kellach unfolded the map from his pocket. "That's where we have to go," he said. "Into the caverns."

CHAPTER

21

Kellach lit the lamp, and he and Moyra entered the cave. The air hung dank and cool—strangled air, edged with coppery odors from deep underground. Air that craved sunlight and freedom.

A draft grazed the back of Kellach's neck, sending a shiver through him. The lamplight threw distorted, flickering orange shadows against the walls.

"Look. Drawings," Moyra said. She ran her fingers along a crude sketch of several stick figures battling brawny, eyeless creatures holding weapons that appeared to be axes.

"Those look like grimlocks," Kellach said, pointing at the eyeless creatures. "The thin figures could be people." The cave swallowed his voice.

"Do you think it's a warning?"

He shrugged. "We have to go into the tunnel." Fear welled in his throat. Fear could be good, he told himself. It would keep him alert.

He led the way deeper into the dark. The lamp threw dancing light and shadows in their path. Soon, the passage opened into another cave.

Moyra gasped.

Two skeletons slumped in the corner, side by side, as if they'd been chatting over tea and had simply died. One was slightly bigger than the other was. Were they siblings? Friends? Parent and child?

The skin, muscles, and sinews had long ago turned to dust. Only dry bones remained, white and sinister in the lamplight. The deep eye sockets stared at nothing. The jaws, devoid of flesh, had frozen in eternal grins.

Moyra crouched next to the remains and touched one of the skulls. She glanced up at Kellach. "The bone is crushed."

Kellach held the lamp near the other skull. "This one too. The arm is broken. They must've been in a battle. They came in here and collapsed. Maybe they died from their injuries—"

"There's something else." Moyra stood and backed away from the bones. "Look closely, Kellach. Tooth marks. The grimlocks. They ate these people." Her face paled.

"It happened a long time ago," Kellach said quickly. Goose bumps raced across his skin. "Grimlocks prefer fresh, raw meat—"

"Preferably human." Moyra shivered. "I don't like this, Kellach. The two of us alone would never win a fight against a bunch of grimlocks."

"We won't have to fight them. They live deep beneath the earth. They haven't been up here in a long time. I'd know if they had."

"But what if we have to go deep beneath the earth too?"

Kellach grabbed her hand. "Look at me, Moyra. We keep our heads. The map will help us. We're here for a reason. We'll make it."

"What if we don't? What if we end up like . . . that? Forgotten skeletons with gnawed bones? Nobody will bury us. Nobody will—"

"We're getting the amulet, and then we're getting out of here." He sounded far more confident than he felt.

For a time, there were only the sounds of their footsteps and breathing. The tunnel meandered, sometimes curving left, sometimes curving right. Soon they came to a fork. Kellach unfolded the map.

"It's too quiet," Moyra whispered. "And I can't stand the low ceiling."

Kellach had to duck to avoid hitting his head. "We take the left passage."

"Are you sure?" Moyra leaned over him to see the map. Her hair, giving off a faint scent of cedar smoke, brushed his arm.

"What? You don't think I'm capable of reading a map?" he said.

"Aren't two heads better than one?"

"You're right." He exhaled. He didn't realize he'd been holding his breath. They were both jittery.

Moyra rummaged in the pack and produced the chalk. "Now I know why we needed this. In case we get lost."

Kellach nodded, and Moyra marked the wall with an arrow. They headed left down another endless passageway. At every juncture, she drew another arrow. Kellach tried to gauge their direction, but he couldn't get a fix.

"We're going downhill," Moyra said. "Can't you feel it?"

Kellach nodded. How much farther down would they go? Into grimlock territory? They came to several more forks, and each time they consulted the map for direction.

Moyra stopped and clutched his arm. She put a finger to her lips. He knew to trust her keen sense of hearing.

"Something's coming," she whispered. "I hear voices. Far down the passage."

"What kinds of voices?" Kellach held up the lamp. "What are they saying?" The light revealed nothing but darkness ahead.

"A garbled language. What if it's the grimlocks?"

Kellach took a deep breath. "Doubtful. Many different creatures live underground. I can't tell at this distance. Are they coming this way?"

Moyra nodded grimly. "Should we go back?"

"We have to go forward for the amulet."

She nodded and led the way. The voices grew louder. Not voices, really. Grunts and snarls.

Two animated silhouettes appeared several yards ahead, where the tunnel opened into a dimly lit cave.

"Stop," Kellach whispered to Moyra. "Stand perfectly still."

She stood motionless, in full view of the creatures. Standing as tall as humans, the two gray shadows, with muscular arms and legs, stringy hair, and pointed ears, growled and fought over some unknown prize. They battled in hand-to-hand combat—perhaps some cultural ritual understood only by a beastlike society tucked deep inside the earth.

"Grimlocks," Kellach whispered in Moyra's ear. He felt her body shudder. "They won't spot us."

She nodded.

Where their eyes should have been, grimlocks had only blank, eyeless sockets.

"How close are we?" Moyra whispered in Kellach's ear.

"I'd say fifty feet."

"At forty feet—"

"I know. They'll smell us."

"We could slip by."

"You know how to be silent, but I don't, and there might be more where they came from. They live in large communities. They only come to the surface to raid for slaves—"

"—or to hunt for fresh meat. I know." Moyra trembled. "These two are hunters on their way out, aren't they?"

"Maybe." He and Moyra backed into the shadows.

"We have to find an alternate route." He unfolded the map as quietly as he could.

Moyra pointed to a convoluted passage on the map. "There's another way, there. It's longer, but it could work."

"Let's do it." Kellach folded the map just as the grimlocks stopped fighting, noses to the air.

They grunted, turned toward Kellach and Moyra, then scrambled for their stone battle-axes.

Moyra was already running. Kellach followed, but heavy footsteps thundered up behind him.

"Duck!" Kellach yelled as the first grimlock swung its axe at Moyra.

She ducked left, then right, avoiding the creature's blind swings.

The second grimlock lunged at Kellach. He jumped aside, dropped the lamp, then grabbed the grimlock's arm and yanked. The monster's skull thudded against the stone wall.

Shaking its head, the fiend took another shot at Kellach. Heart pounding, Kellach tried to chant an obscure spell, but he couldn't concentrate. The lamp lay on the ground, giving off a halo of light.

This close, the grimlocks' exceptional senses of smell and hearing made them formidable foes. Moyra ducked and kicked, hopping and bobbing. Kellach punched one grimlock, sending it reeling backward. The axe clattered to the ground. When the second grimlock attacked, Moyra and Kellach each grabbed an arm and pulled, and the monster hit the wall and slumped. But it wouldn't be down for long.

"Look! Two more are coming." Moyra pointed back toward the cave.

"I have an idea." Kellach fumbled in the bag, and he pulled out a small vial. "Here put this on. You only need a few drops." Kellach dabbed the oil on his neck.

Moyra wrinkled her nose as she grabbed the little bottle. "Perfume? Won't this just make them smell us more easily?"

Kellach shook his head. "It's concealing perfume! Instead of making an odor, it masks odors. I found it in Mom's hope chest. I'm sure she meant for us to find it." Kellach glanced down the corridor and began to run ahead. "Quickly! Put it on!" Moyra dabbed a few drops on her wrist, then ran after Kellach down the winding tunnel.

The grimlocks followed the sound of their footsteps, moving slowly with their noses to the ground.

"They hear us, but they no longer smell our human odor," Kellach whispered. "With the oil, they won't smell us at all!"

"This way." Moyra turned right. The passage widened and grew damper. Somewhere in the distance, water dripped from the ceiling.

Now we can only hope, Kellach thought as the grimlocks turned down the passage, their noses to the ground.

CHAPTER

22

Kellach snuffed out the lamp's flame. The heat would be a dead giveaway. He chanted the spell to summon darkvision.

"What are you doing?" Moyra whispered. Her face appeared white in the gloom.

"I'm conjuring the ability to see without light. It's the only way to get us out of here."

"Can you give me darkvision too?" She stared blindly into blackness, her face tight with fear.

"I'll have to be the eyes for both of us. I promise . . . everything will be okay." Kellach wasn't so sure, but he had to believe. His heart tapped a rapid staccato beat. If the grimlocks turned, if the perfume didn't work and they caught even a whiff of human scent, all would be lost. "Shhh . . . they're coming."

The first three grimlocks trod toward them. Kellach held his breath for what seemed like an eternity as they sauntered past. The fourth grimlock stopped right in front of him.

Please, please, go away, Kellach thought.

The grimlock raised its head and turned, staring directly at Kellach through empty eye sockets. Unnerved, Kellach held his breath. The grimlock kept staring.

It can't see me; it can't see me, Kellach told himself in a silent mantra. It has no eyes.

Moyra stood motionless, her back pressed against the wall. The grimlock faced Kellach for several moments, then crouched and followed the other grimlocks down the tunnel.

Kellach let out a long breath, and Moyra gasped. He took her hand and they dashed back the way they had come. There was no sound of grimlocks following, but Kellach knew the lull wouldn't last. He slowed for a moment to relight the lamp. Soon they seemed to be climbing up through the mountain. Moyra held the map and pointed the way at each juncture.

"We're here," she said finally at the mouth of a vast, dark cavern. They both stopped to catch their breath.

Everburning torches, mounted on wall sconces, gave off only feeble illumination. Who had lit them? Intricate murals depicted misty forests, bubbling streams, deer, and wildflowers.

Massive chairs and tables lay on the floor—some intact, some broken. A faint scent of rotting wood rose into the dank air.

The cave walls climbed perhaps a hundred feet and curved into a dome-shaped ceiling. The murals extended across the top. At the opposite end of the cave, another arched entrance yawned into blackness.

"According to the map, the amulet is in a box somewhere

in here—against the far wall," Moyra said. "Strange that it's not guarded."

"Our map is the only map. Nobody knows about the amulet. Nobody except Nahemah and my mom."

"Do you suppose Nahemah's here?"

"I don't think so," Kellach said. "She doesn't know where to go." Kellach's voice echoed as he stepped into the stadium-sized cave.

"This is no grimlock lair," Moyra said in a shaky voice. "Paintings on the ceiling . . . This must be the home of stone giants. They love to create things. The tables and chairs are stone-giant style. But what happened to the giants?"

"Maybe they abandoned this lair, but I doubt it. Maybe they're out gathering food. Strange, though. Stone giants prefer to live in caves high on rocky, storm-swept mountains, not in underground caverns."

Kellach thought of the pictures Zendric had shown him of tall, lean, hairless creatures resembling humans with smooth, gray skin. Stone skin. Gaunt features and sunken black eyes made stone giants appear grim and dangerous. Standing about twelve feet tall and weighing some 1,500 pounds, most stone giants were unusually playful and artistic.

"Maybe after the Sundering, they *had* to live here," Moyra said. "Maybe evil drove them into hiding. Aren't stone giants shy and gentle?"

"True—most of them pose no threat." Kellach lowered his voice to a whisper. "But I don't think these are ordinary giants."

"What are they then? How do you know?" She shivered, crossing her arms over her chest.

"I feel it. These giants have turned to wickedness. Their corruption swirls all around me. Perhaps their nearness to the Amulet of Power tainted them."

"What if they come back?"

"We run."

"We have to hurry then." Moyra set off through the cave. The room was so large, her form diminished as she sprinted ahead. Kellach caught up.

"Look for an indentation, a shelf," Kellach said when they reached the opposite side of the cave. They ran their fingers along the rough stone, feeling for any small dent or ledge. The minutes ticked away, and Kellach's throat tightened with impatience. The giants could return at any moment.

"Here." Moyra pointed up toward a high ledge. She ran her slender hands along the wall. "I can't climb. No holds."

"I'll levitate you."

"No, save your spells. Boost me."

Kellach hoisted her up. She wasn't too heavy, but he had to concentrate to keep from dropping her. If anyone could scale the wall, Moyra could.

"I still can't reach. Wait. I have an idea. Help me with a chair." She jumped down, and together they managed to drag a giant chair toward the wall. The legs made a loud scraping sound across the stone floor. The chair was so large that both Kellach and Moyra could stand on its seat. Kellach boosted Moyra again. He focused on keeping his balance.

"Just a little higher," she said.

He strained to lift her.

"A little higher."

"I can't. Hurry! I'm going to drop you. The chair is creaking. I think it might break—"

"Wait, wait—"

That was when the cave began to shake, as if a distant earthquake rolled through the mountain. "The giants are coming," Kellach said.

"I almost have it."

"Moyra—"

"Okay. Let me down."

The chair toppled over, and they both tumbled to the ground. Moyra held a smooth, golden box that glowed with an inner white light. Kellach scrambled to his feet. "This is it. The Amulet—"

"We have to be sure."

"Don't open the—"

"Look at the stone. It's beautiful!" Moyra exclaimed. She had already opened the box. The amber amulet, the size of a fist, lay in a bed of red velvet. A deceptively benign gem, the edges formed clean, straight lines that reflected shards of rainbow light. A curious, faint melody played in the distance. The round, sweet notes transported Kellach to a field of fragrant roses. Nahemah waved in the distance. He longed to reach her. The gem called from its center to its next mistress: the woman who would hold dominion over the world.

A hollow, dark hunger seized him. His fingers itched to

grab the gem and hold it close to his chest. He longed to possess it, to own it.

"What do we do with it?" Moyra's innocent voice cut through his trance.

He slammed the box shut. "We take it back to my mom," he said.

"We have to get rid of it!"

"There's no way to destroy it, unless Nahemah fails to recite the spell."

"We could hide the amulet until Zendric returns," Moyra said. "He'll know what to do. As long as *we* have the amulet, she doesn't."

"There's nothing Zendric can do, Moyra. The amulet is already calling to Nahemah. She'll come for it. We have to take it to my mom. She'll help us."

"She's in a trance, Kellach, I don't know. She could summon Nahemah."

"Mom's strong, Moyra. She broke through the trance for a moment. Besides, I think maybe we're meant to draw Nahemah to the amulet. Don't you see? As long as this amulet exists, Nahemah will come looking for it. The two are linked. She has to recite the spell and fail, and then she and the amulet will be destroyed."

Moyra grabbed Kellach's arm. Her lips quivered. "What if she succeeds? What if we can't stop her?"

The cold, dank air traveled up through Kellach's legs and chilled his bones. "Don't you think I've thought of that? I dread what might happen. But do we want Nahemah wandering the realm, destroying innocent people with her deadly charisma? I have to try the secret page spell while she's reciting the silver spell. She has to believe she's in control, and then—"

"She *is* in control." Moyra paced, tapping her teeth with her forefinger. "What if there's another way to destroy the amulet? Throw it into a fire, or—"

"You heard what the book said. There's no other way. We're running out of time. Come on." He was already jogging back across the cave when the rumbling grew louder.

"Kellach!" Moyra tugged Kellach's sleeve and he whipped around. Three giants stumbled in, enormous gray boulders cut into the shapes of men. Kellach froze.

The giants spotted the glowing box and let out a great roar. They lunged forward, each stride covering several feet of ground.

"Come on, Kellach. Run!"

They raced forward. The giants roared up behind them, closing fast.

"Kellach! The palette!" Moyra shouted. "The oil paints! They weren't for us. They were for the giants. They'll do anything for their art."

"Brilliant, Moyra." Kellach fumbled in the bag for the paints, then turned and threw the box. It hit a giant in the knee and clattered to the floor.

The giants gathered around the paint. The tallest giant picked up the box and dipped a finger into the paint, then exclaimed in awe.

"Usually they have to make their own paints from plants,"

Kellach whispered. "They're thrilled. This will buy us a few minutes."

He and Moyra dashed to the entrance. Ahead in the hall, the grimlocks advanced, blocking the way.

Kellach and Moyra backed into the cave and dashed behind a table that had fallen on its side.

Moyra glanced up and ran her fingers along the wall.

"You're not seriously thinking of climbing," Kellach said.

"If we get above their heads, they can't reach us."

"I'm not a climber. And what happens when we reach the ceiling? There's no way out."

"Can you make a door?"

"Not fast enough. The rock must be several feet thick here."

"Then what do we do?"

"I don't know, Moyra. I don't know!"

"I know," Moyra whispered. "Make us invisible like you did with the cloak. The amulet too."

"The grimlocks will smell us—"

"They'll also smell the giants, and the giants won't see us."

"Okay. Hang on."

The giants still gathered around the paint. They cooed and exclaimed as if the paint palette were a newborn giant baby.

Just as the grimlocks burst in cursing, Kellach focused on the glowing box and chanted an invisibility spell. The giants bellowed and raced forward. The paint palette fell and broke on the floor.

The grimlocks raised their battle-axes, and the giants

wielded their clubs. The two armies rushed at each other. The grimlocks growled and attacked in vicious abandon, while the giants shouted and swung their clubs with grace and power.

Kellach tried to tune out the furor.

Concentrate, boy, you can do it.

Kellach focused. Slowly, his hands disappeared, then Moyra's legs, then her torso, then his legs. His head hurt from the strain. A fierce ringing sound pierced his eardrums. Moyra gasped, looking down at her fading body. The box grew fuzzy and then vanished as the giants clashed with the grimlocks. The great *whump* of clubs striking battle-axes filled the air. The cave shook, and then Moyra and Kellach disappeared altogether.

CHAPTER

23

Kellach sensed his body and knew it was there. He could touch his arm and his legs, but they were made of solid, transparent matter. He could breathe and think and feel, but his corporeal body was invisible.

"It worked," Moyra whispered. "But this feels so weird. Where am I? Where are you?"

"You're there. I'm here." He reached out and touched a warm, firm surface. Her arm. He took her hand. "Don't let go. Come on."

They crawled along the edge of the room, keeping to the wall. One grimlock, in the heat of battle, glanced in their direction, then swung its battle-axe at a giant and chopped off its finger. The finger flew through the air and landed at Kellach's feet. The muscles trembled and smoke rose from the skin, and then the finger lay still. Moyra gasped.

The giant screamed and swung its club at the grimlock. The creatures locked in earnest battle, knocking over tables, breaking chairs, and banging into walls.

Only a few more paces. Kellach sidestepped the giant finger. He hardly dared to breathe. He grabbed the lamp from where he'd dropped it on the floor, and then he and Moyra reached the doorway, slipped out into the passage, and ran.

They remained invisible for several minutes as they retraced their steps. Racing along, they followed Moyra's chalked arrows. The passage curved right, then left, descended for eons, then climbed again.

None of the monsters followed. The shouts and banging from the giants' lair diminished in the distance. Soon, the monsters would either kill each other or forget their hostilities and realize the box was gone. The grimlocks had not tried to steal the amulet, or they would've fought the giants for the gem long ago. Perhaps only the giants knew only that the gem could be valuable. Perhaps they protected it the way they might protect a cache of diamonds. Kellach would never know what the giants thought, and he wasn't about to go back and find out.

Kellach used the lamp until the invisibility spell began to wear off. Then the box reappeared to light the way with its unearthly glow.

Kellach's body rematerialized in bits and pieces. One foot, the other thigh, then his left arm. Moyra's face appeared in brushstrokes, then her mane of red hair, then her legs.

"This is creepy. I don't have arms." She waved her hands, which seemed to dance by themselves in the air.

"I know—spooky." Kellach tried to keep his voice from shaking. He hadn't known his own power. He still didn't feel comfortable casting such extreme spells. "We'll be ourselves again in no time, I hope."

"We'd better be. I don't want to be half-Moyra forever, a severed head and hands floating around scaring people."

"You won't, I promise." But he wasn't at all sure.

CHAPTER

24

On their way out, they passed the two skeletons again. The remains hadn't moved, although Kellach sensed the bones crumbling, slaves to the ravages of time. Moyra knelt next to the skeletons and left a small token—the dandelion from her pocket. It brought a splash of color to the darkness. "You won't be forgotten," she said quietly, and she and Kellach stood in silent tribute to the two lost souls.

"We have to go," Kellach said.

Outside the caves, they squinted in the brightness. The forest quieted, as if all creatures cringed and watched in awe as Kellach and Moyra traced the path homeward, back to the chaos of Curston. He put the box into his pack.

The return journey passed without incident. No grimlocks, no athachs, no giants.

As Kellach and Moyra slipped in through the Oldgate, a blank-eyed Torin greeted them. "What are you two doing?" he asked in a flat voice. "Where have you been?"

The blood drained from Kellach's cheeks. He glanced at Moyra. "We've just come from the dangerous caves to the south," he said.

"Don't you know you shouldn't be out after dark?" The pupils of Torin's eyes were dilated. He scratched a few days' growth of beard, and his clothes hung loose and wrinkled as if he'd slept in them. His sword dangled unsharp and useless at his side.

"It's not dark, Dad," Kellach said, fear and pity hitting him in the gut. "What's wrong with you?" He took his father by the shoulders and shook him. Torin submitted without struggle, his head flopping forward.

"He's in Nahemah's trance, Kellach. Stop." Moyra tugged Kellach's arm and pulled him down the road. Kellach glanced back over his shoulder. Torin still stood in a trance.

Anger roiled inside Kellach, and he bit back tears. Boys don't cry. Men don't cry, he told himself. He hated Nahemah then. He hated her with all his heart. If it weren't for her, Torin, Breddo, Driskoll, Jourdain—everyone would be okay.

"Look at this place." Moyra held her nose as they picked their way through piles of garbage. A stale, sour scent lingered in the air, a mixture of rotting meat, vomit, and excrement. A few men meandered among stray dogs, cats, chickens, and goats. Otherwise, the city was deserted.

"Where is everyone?" Moyra whispered. She stuck to the shadows along the edge of the road.

"Hiding or staring into space, I bet." Kellach glanced up at blank, indifferent windows. Evil hung like dirty laundry in every garden. Eyes followed them from behind curtains, from hidden corners. The closer they got to home, the more Kellach knew he was being watched.

"We have to pretend everything's normal and that we've just been out in the city having fun," Kellach said.

"I can't pretend—"

"You have to."

"All right. I'll try." Moyra bit her lip, and they went inside Kellach's back door. Kellach's jaw dropped in shock. The house was in disarray. Dishes filled the sink, food littered the countertops, and flies buzzed over the refuse bin. An odor of stuffiness invaded the air.

Kellach's stomach flipped. He hoped Driskoll and Jourdain were okay.

"What's going on here?" Moyra screwed up her nose.

"Act normal," Kellach whispered pointing toward the ceiling. The floor creaked upstairs. He was sure Nahemah waited there. What was she doing? Sucking the life force from Driskoll and Jourdain?

Kellach climbed the stairs, with Moyra in tow. A plank squeaked beneath his shoe. Near his bedroom door, he put a finger to his lips, and Moyra stopped behind him.

In the bedroom, Driskoll laughed, and Jourdain spoke in a low lilting voice. Driskoll replied, his voice airy and loving and curiously dronelike.

Kellach breathed a long sigh of relief.

"It's just Mom and Driskoll," he said, then pushed the door open. "She seems to be a bit better."

Jourdain was bent over Driskoll's bed, tucking the covers under the mattress. Driskoll's blank, black eyes gazed at her in adoration.

She turned, straightened, and smiled at Kellach. Worry edged her blue eyes. "Kellach, darling. Where have you been? I was so worried. I thought you'd been hurt or even killed. Why didn't you tell me where you were going?"

"Mom. I, uh—" His vocal chords constricted. His mother's kind, deep blue eyes drew him. "You're not in a trance!"

"I heard your voice through a fog, Kellach." She touched his cheek. "I wandered through a dark wood. Only burned trees with gnarled limbs surrounded me. I heard you calling, telling me to fight Nahemah. I followed the sound. You pulled me from a dream."

"Mom, I'm so glad you're okay." Kellach's heart filled with tenderness.

"Of course she's okay," Driskoll said. "She's a wizard. She can fight Nahemah."

"Where *is* Nahemah?" Moyra asked. She'd been hanging back in the doorway and now stepped into the room.

"Waiting for the amulet." Jourdain glanced toward the window, and her brows furrowed. "We must be prepared to face her."

Kellach thought of the curly-haired woman dancing in the Skinned Cat, and his mind went fuzzy again. "I don't know if I can fend her off this time," he said. Suddenly, his arms and legs grew heavy, and his eyelids drooped.

"Come, sit," Jourdain said. "You both must be cold and

hungry. Shall I make you a bowl of soup?"

"We went after the amulet," Moyra said, pacing the room. "Kellach has it."

Jourdain's eyes widened. "How did you know about the amulet?"

"You told us! And a book told us." Kellach related the visit to the library.

"Kellach!" Jourdain gasped and stood. "Why didn't you come to me? Such a journey into the caves is terribly dangerous!"

"We know, and we're fine, as you can see!" Moyra grinned.

"We found the map in the mirror," Kellach said. "The one you left for me, with instructions."

"Ah, yes, the map!" Jourdain pressed her fingers to her forehead.

"The map saved us," Kellach said.

Driskoll clicked his tongue in annoyance. "What's all this talk about maps and amulets? I'm hungry!"

Kellach dropped his backpack on the bed.

"I'll cook supper soon," Jourdain said. "Moyra, my darling girl. What's happened to you?"

Kellach turned to Moyra. She stared ahead, eyes glazed.

"Moyra's in a trance," he said, and now his head filled with cotton. "Nahemah . . . must be . . . near. She must sense the . . . amulet." He had trouble thinking and speaking. Moyra was supposed to be the strong one.

Moyra, Kellach thought. Say something. Help me.

Jourdain pulled him down to sit beside her. "My dear boy, the last time you looked so pale, you'd just seen a half-orc run naked through Main Square. Do you remember? You were only four and quite impressionable."

"Mom . . . Nahemah's near."

"Give me the amulet, and we'll keep it safe from her." Jourdain stroked his hair and touched his forehead with a cool, gentle hand. "My goodness! You're burning with fever."

Strange images flooded his brain. He remembered playing hide-and-seek in the street with his friends. Then his mother called him inside for supper, and his friends came too. He was a child again, frolicking in safety beneath a benevolent sun. His father's eyes had been warm and kind in those days . . . Now . . . where was he? Kellach knew he had to remember . . .

He allowed Moyra to open the pack on the bed.

"Now, my dear girl," Jourdain said. "Be careful. Don't stare directly at the amulet for too long, or its evil will capture you. Will you give it to me?"

"Moyra, be careful!" Kellach heard his voice from very far away, but he couldn't bring it closer. He couldn't move. He sat on the bed, his legs and arms leaden. He had a dreadful urge to lie down and sleep, to hear his mother's lullaby.

Moyra pulled out the box. What was inside? Something important. Something, but what?

"Now open the box and hand me the amulet," Jourdain said. "Very carefully."

Moyra opened the box. The gem gave off a surreal glow that lit her face and hair. Her eyes widened as she gazed at the glowing stone.

"You've done very well," Jourdain said softly. "You and Kellach are true Knights of the Silver Dragon."

Kellach's chest filled with warmth. He was a Knight, a Knight . . . of what?

Moyra handed over the amulet.

Kellach used all his strength to raise his arms, and then they fell to his sides again.

Driskoll watched impassively from his bed.

"Thank you, my dears," Jourdain said. "Now you've done all you can do."

"We have to destroy it," Kellach managed to say.

Moyra stood in a hypnotic trance. Her fingers curled into fists at her sides, and she swayed slightly.

"Of course," Jourdain said. "Now I must recite the silver spell to destroy the amulet."

"No, Mom," Kellach said. "The silver spell will give the amulet holder the full power of evil!"

"Is that so? I'll gain the full power of evil—"

"Nahemah will."

"Nahemah's not here, so I should forge ahead." She raised one eyebrow. Her eyes were black marbles, and her hair turned a shade darker. Her complexion paled, and the soft lines of her face hardened into sharp planes.

"Mom, what's wrong with you?" Kellach's throat tightened. An invisible frost raised all the hairs on his skin. He found his legs and scrambled back against the wall.

Jourdain was changing.

Her shining blond hair darkened to raven strands. She grew

taller, her body elongating, her breasts bulging, and two enormous black, webbed wings spread from her back.

Her face altered, the lower jaw growing harder, the nose sharp and long, the eyes bright, piercing violet. Her skin turned pale green. Her charisma breathed through the room.

CHAPTER

25

"Yyou're not my mother!" Kellach shook himself, trying to free his mind from the trance. "You're Nahemah!"

"I'm glad you've finally learned my name," Nahemah said. "You've simplified my life. Imagine—you found the map and the amulet, and I didn't have to lift a finger. I did not want to befoul myself fighting ridiculous athachs, grimlocks, and stone giants. Good thing you survived, otherwise where would my amulet be? Still gathering dust in that useless cavern, no doubt. What a waste."

"You knew," Kellach said. "Moyra . . . "

"Oh, she's no help to you now." Nahemah waved a dismissive wing toward Moyra. "She was useful while you two puttered about in those caves, making fools of yourselves. I'm glad the little twit can climb, or you might never have found the amulet."

Kellach couldn't move. Spots danced before his eyes. "You . . . knew. You . . . knew everything that happened to us."

"Of course I knew. Do you think I'd have let you go without knowing what you were up against? I have to admit that I thought you both might die. Then I would've had an inconvenient mess to clean up. I would have sent Driskoll in your place. He has a fair amount of courage, but he would've needed you for the spells . . . I could have sent Torin, I suppose—"

Driskoll lay on his bed, eyes still black and vacant.

"I should have known," Kellach said. "When you returned to Curston, I knew something was wrong. I didn't know what until now. You sent us the note. You signed it 'Mother.' Our real mother would never have signed a note that way. She would've signed it 'Mom.'"

"A minor mistake!"

"You forgot how old Driskoll was, and you forgot that Curston was once called Promise."

"Promise, Curston, what does it matter?" Nahemah shouted. "Who cares how old Driskoll is?"

"When I saw wings in my mind, they were yours!"

"And aren't they beautiful?" She spread her webbed wings, and foul smell hit Kellach's nostrils.

"You were the curly-haired woman with freckles—"

"And Royma. I encountered Breddo as I entered Curston, and Royma was most vivid in his mind. So I decided to become her for a while."

"And that means . . ." Kellach glanced at his bed. Jourdain's spellbook and the blue cloak lay in a neat pile on his pillow. "The blue cloak! You never took it from my mom . . . You had it all along!"

Nahemah chuckled. "Yes, and it was most annoying of you to steal it from me. Luckily, dear Driskoll's thoughts guided me right to it. Clever of you to hide the cloak and the spellbook together like that. It made my work so much easier!"

"When Zendric returns, he'll kill you," Kellach said.

"Ha, Zendric." Nahemah cackled. "A useless old crow, if I ever saw one."

"He's not useless. He could banish you with a thought."

Nahemah leaned in close, and her voice grew guttural and harsh. "Yes, but he's not here, is he? He's off tending to Ssarine, whom I made very ill."

"You made Ssarine ill? You harmed Locky too!"

"How else could I get rid of your allies? That troublesome dragon was pestering me. He deserved the beating I gave him. And Zendric? He would've known right away who I was, and then the game would've been up, right? I'm no idiot, boy. Now that I hold the amulet, I hold the key to power over all of humanity. The gem will call forth the Abyss—"

"I won't let you do this!" Kellach struggled to his feet, then stumbled.

"Of course you will. You did all the work for me." She held the amulet up to the light. Her wings flapped. "Oh, most beautiful gem, creator of all power, you will serve me well. You will unite the Abyss with Curston, and all creatures of darkness shall come forth into the light—"

"No!" Kellach reached into his mind and grabbed desperately at any remaining spells. He tried to obscure the amulet, but he couldn't concentrate. He tried to wrench it

from Nahemah's grip. He failed. He tried to shove her with his mind and tried to make the amulet very small, but his mind lay feeble, a useless, blunt instrument.

"Stop!" he shouted, but his voice came out a whisper.

"Hush, boy." Nahemah held Jourdain's spellbook in one hand and the amulet in the other. "And now, the power of all worlds will be mine." She opened the book to the silver spell and began to recite in a sharp screech that sliced into Kellach's nerves.

"You won't succeed," he said again, but he wasn't sure he'd spoken. He tried to step forward to grab the spellbook, but instead he fell to his knees.

CHAPTER

26

Kellach struggled to stay awake. The urge to sleep coiled around him and squeezed.

Zendric's angry face hovered behind his eyelids. *Concentrate. One day, your life may depend on it.*

Using every ounce of strength and training, Kellach shoved Nahemah's spell from his mind. He imagined her charm as a black ball of death and hurled the ball out of his head. His eyelids fluttered open. His thoughts sharpened, but he couldn't move.

Moyra stood motionless, facing the window. The wind howled, rattled the panes, and scattered debris. Monsters roared in the distance. Curston folded in upon itself. Heavy air, cursed with the reek of decay, swirled in and careened around the room.

Nahemah still held the spellbook and the amulet as she recited the silver spell. The sound reminded Kellach of crawling maggots, rotting meat, and the dirty underside of rocks.

Driskoll sat upright in bed. His pupils were no longer dilated.

He stared clear-eyed at Nahemah, and his lips turned down. Kellach tried to reach out and strained to speak, but he couldn't. Something was happening to Driskoll. His muscles tensed, and his mouth quivered with anger.

Kellach shook his head to steady his thoughts. He was supposed to do something, to *know* something. But what?

The silver spell. Silver. Why was it written in silver? Reflections. Mirrors. The mirror!

He remembered what the book had told them: *She avoids direct sunlight and mirrors, which magnify and reflect her evil upon herself.*

He turned, straining to reach the mirror in the closet, but his legs cleaved to the floor like tree roots. His body wouldn't move.

"You're not our mother!" Driskoll's shout cut through Nahemah's deadening voice. "You don't sound like her. You don't even look like her anymore. You're green, and you have wings!"

She threw her head back and laughed, a great cackle that made the walls shudder. "You've only just now seen the truth? Now you've interrupted me and I shall have to begin again."

"What have you done with our mother?" Driskoll shouted.

"I've done nothing with her. Granted, I would have if I could. You see, my story was partially true—I did find your mother and imprison her for a time. She escaped, but it wasn't a total loss. I gleaned many memories from her mind—"

"Is she alive?" Kellach asked. "Where is she?"

"I haven't a clue, and I don't care."

Kellach's heart folded in with sadness. Where was Jourdain? She had never been there and had never touched his forehead. His happiness, the feeling of a family—it had all been an illusion. He fought back tears.

"Our mom's stronger than you are," Driskoll said. "She's a real wizard. You tricked us. You—"

"I did nothing of the kind," Nahemah shrieked, nearly dropping the spellbook. "You tricked yourself. You wanted to see your mother, and that is whom you saw."

"But you knew about the spellbook, you knew—"

"I have my methods."

"Our mom will find you and destroy you!" Driskoll's fingers tightened into trembling fists. Moyra didn't move. Kellach stared at Driskoll. How had he broken the spell?

Nahemah waved the hand holding the amulet. Shards of brilliant amber light danced across the walls. "Destroy me? Ha! Your mother is probably wandering off in another plane, some other dimension. She's forgotten you."

"She would never forget us," Driskoll said.

Nahemah ignored him and began reciting the spell from the beginning.

"Everything you knew about us," Driskoll went on. "Everything you said—"

"Was a lie!" Kellach shouted. "Driskoll—"

"I know what to do." In an instant, Driskoll lunged for the closet, grabbed the mirror, and held it up to Nahemah.

The amulet's light bounced off the glass and reflected in

her eyes. She let out a spine-shattering scream, so unearthly that even the wind stopped howling. The world stopped spinning, and the clouds stopped roiling.

"Driskoll. Don't look at her. Don't look into her eyes! She'll mesmerize you!" Kellach yelled. Moyra blinked, slowly returning to normal.

Driskoll held the mirror to Nahemah and closed his eyes.

The light seared her skin, sending flames across her cheek. She screamed. The stench of burning flesh filled the air.

"Keep the mirror focused on her!" Kellach said. His mind grew sharper.

"It's working!" Driskoll said.

Nahemah clung to the amulet and spellbook as the edges of her wings caught fire, then her hair.

She recited faster, racing to finish the spell. Her skin burned as she narrated the silver spell. The amulet began to glow. She held the gem in front of her, warding off her searing reflection.

Then the mirror shattered and slipped from Driskoll's hand. He jumped back as the pieces rained to the floor.

"Hah, silly children!" Nahemah screeched. Her left eye had melted into her cheek. "Did you think you could stop me so easily?"

27

Nahemah's power grew stronger with every line she read. Her skin glowed. Her right eye shone bright violet.

"What do we do now?" Driskoll shouted. "Kellach!"

"The amulet protects her!" Kellach said. "But the more energy she uses to recite the spell, the weaker her charisma becomes. Moyra!"

Moyra snapped to full attention and whipped around. She lunged for Nahemah, only to be repelled by an invisible force.

Moyra flew back and thudded against the wall. "Kellach!" she yelled. "Do something. Remember the secret page spell. That's all that can save us now!"

The incantation to hide the silver spell! The only one he couldn't get right. He had to try. He searched his memory. "I can't remember the words."

"Yes, you can," Driskoll said. "If I can break Nahemah's hold, you can too. She can't keep you under her spell if you don't *believe* she can. She can only put a kid in a trance, if you let her. I wanted to *believe* she was Mom. When I finally saw that she was Nahemah—" His voice broke. "Come on, Kellach. You can do it—"

"Okay, okay. Wait." He remembered the first words and recited them, softly at first, then louder. "It's not working." Nahemah's voice boomed loud enough to shatter the heavens.

"I can't do it," Kellach said.

"Try again," Moyra screamed. "You can do it. You can." She held her nose against the stink of smoldering hair and skin.

"We know you can," Driskoll said. "You have to succeed. For Curston."

"For your dad. For my dad," Moyra said.

Kellach tried again. He tuned out the flames, the succubus, her singed wings flapping, the amulet, and his mother's spell-book. Nothing happened. Nahemah had almost finished reciting the spell.

No.

He conjured an image of Zendric in a gentle moment of recollection, his wise eyes bright with tears as he remembered Jourdain.

For you, Mom, Kellach thought.

He recited the secret page spell one last time.

Nahemah screamed. She dropped the spellbook, and Kellach caught it in midair and held it close to his chest.

"What have you done?" she screeched as her whole body burst into flames. Her shrieks would reverberate in Kellach's head for years to come. "You've ruined everything. You've destroyed me!"

"Be gone, Nahemah!" Kellach yelled.

Moyra crouched in the corner, her hands over her ears. Driskoll slid down against the wall. Nahemah was melting, her hair falling off in clumps and the skin dripping from her bones. The reek made Kellach gag. He broke out in a sweat. Driskoll fell into a fit of coughing.

Nahemah brandished the amulet like a weapon, and then her hand and the amulet burst into flames. In a great surge of smoke, she exploded and showered to the ground in smoldering embers.

Ashes flew and lodged in Kellach's eyelashes. He brushed Nahemah off his clothes. Driskoll coughed, and Moyra sneezed several times.

"Is she gone? Is she gone for good?" Moyra shook ashes from her hair.

"I think so." Kellach prodded the smoking, charred remains. The ashes sizzled in a pile on the floor.

The sky brightened outside, and the wind died. The room fell quiet.

Kellach, Driskoll, and Moyra stared at the mess where Nahemah had stood.

Driskoll's face softened with sadness. "She wasn't really Mom," he said mournfully.

"It's okay, Driskoll." Kellach draped an arm around his brother's shoulders.

Moyra rushed forward and hugged both of them. "You did it. Driskoll, you were amazing. Kellach . . . you're a great wizard."

"We couldn't have done it without you, Moyra," Kellach said. He blushed.

"Look!" Driskoll pointed. Something glinted in the pile of ashes. Kellach dug through the debris and produced the burnt remains of the amulet, now a tiny, jagged piece of blackened stone. A small remnant of amber glittered in the center, about the size of a fingernail. A souvenir.

CHAPTER

28

K ellach awoke to sunshine and the sound of laughter outside. Curston bustled with early morning market activity. The scent of newly baked bread wafted up through the window.

He rubbed the sleep from his eyes, then memory rushed in and his heart fell. His mother wasn't waiting downstairs. She'd never been here at all.

On the nightstand, the tiny piece of charred amulet glinted, a reminder that he hadn't been stuck in a nightmare. Nahemah had really been there.

Kellach got up to wash and dress. No time for moping. He tucked the shard of amulet into his pocket and went downstairs. Driskoll and Torin sat at the dining table, devouring a breakfast of golden toast and juice. Torin was back to his usual, stiff self, dressed in the pressed garments of captain of the watch, his sword in the scabbard by his side.

"I dreamed of your mother," he said, rubbing his temples.

"She was so real. I recall bits and pieces, but they don't make sense. Strange."

I dreamed of her too, Kellach thought with sadness. If only she could've returned. If only—

"She was real, but she wasn't Mom," Driskoll said, slurping his juice. "She was a succubus."

Torin frowned and shoveled toast into his mouth. "A succubus, eh? Your imagination running away with you again?"

Kellach sat across from Driskoll and gave him a warning look. "You were dreaming, Dad."

Torin dropped the fork on his plate with a clatter. "My dreams have rarely been so vivid. Filled me with hope. Perhaps your mother is trying to find her way home."

Kellach's eyes stung with tears. He blinked them away. "We all have dreams, Dad, but we must also live in reality."

Torin scraped his plate clean and stood. "Ah, Kellach. Older than your years, and so sure of yourself. Just like your mother."

"I dreamed of her too," Driskoll said. "Maybe you're right, Dad. Maybe one day she'll find her way home."

"Let's hope so, son." Torin tried to sound nonchalant, but Kellach detected a waver in his voice. "Off to work. Be good." And he was gone, as if nothing had transpired. As if Nahemah had never existed.

Things were supposed to be this way, Kellach thought. Life was supposed to return to normal. He sat across from his brother. "How much do you remember?"

"Not much, but I know I was in a trance. I know I said things I shouldn't have said. I'm sorry."

"It's okay. We all say things we regret. You weren't yourself."

"I still wish she could've been Mom. I miss her."

"So do I, Driskoll."

"I'm sorry, Kellach. Sorry I didn't go with you to get the amulet. I could've helped. With my sword, I could've fought the athachs, the grimlocks—"

"Wasn't your fault. Nahemah had you under her spell—"

"Because I wanted Mom to be here. My desire fed Nahemah's power. I was weak."

"Missing Mom isn't a weakness. I wish I could've shielded you, but I wasn't strong enough. I should've prevented Nahemah from hypnotizing you. I wish—"

"She hypnotized the whole city, didn't she? You saved me. You saved everyone."

"No, you did. You were great with that mirror." Kellach tried to smile.

Moyra burst in rosy-cheeked. She rushed around to hug first Driskoll, then Kellach. She smelled of cinnamon and soap.

"My dad's back to normal," she said in a breathless voice. "The whole city is awake. They're cleaning up and fixing everything. We did it."

"Of course we did," Kellach said. He wished he felt happier.

"And Zendric's back."

"Zendric? Is he okay?" Kellach's heart lifted.

"Of course he's okay. Come on." The three of them ran outside, leaving half-eaten breakfast on the table, and headed for Zendric's tower. The streets hummed with life. In Main Square, traveling musicians kicked up a lively dance tune.

Merchants set up their booths, and shopkeepers swept the gutters and picked up debris. A chorus of hammers and saws rang through the air as contractors repaired walls, windows, and doors.

Members of the watch patrolled the streets with vigilance. Most heartening of all, there were no zombies milling about in a trance. Kellach found solace in seeing bright-eyed, alert friends shouting, singing, and arguing.

In his tower, Zendric strutted around, cleaning up the mess. Books flew back onto the shelves, and animated brooms swept the floors. Lochinvar shone as if new and flitted about, straightening scrolls and picking up bits of broken glass. He tweeted and floated to Moyra when he saw her. "Moy-ra—friend."

"Locky! How are you feeling?" She wrapped her arms awkwardly around the dragon's rotund metal torso.

Locky tweeted in reply, then whirred to Kellach and alighted on his shoulder. Kellach's heart warmed. "It's great to have you whole again, Locky."

"What kind of name is that?" Zendric asked grumpily. "Locky?"

"What would you name him?"

"How about 'Pain in the Backside'? Took ages to repair the darned contraption."

The dragonet tweeted. "Lochin-var is not con-trap-tion."

"Dragonet then," Zendric said.

"Thank-you for re-pairing me."

"You're welcome." Zendric frowned at the dragonet, then enveloped the children in a great wizard's hug. "So good to see

172

you, my friends." He pulled back. "What's happened here?"

None of them spoke. They looked at one another.

"How are you? How's Ssarine?" Kellach asked finally. He was filled to nearly bursting with the story of Nahemah.

"She's fine . . . now." But Zendric's voice shook.

"She was really sick, wasn't she?" Kellach said.

Zendric nodded. "Then suddenly she made a dramatic improvement, as if a spell had been broken."

"It was Nahemah's spell," Driskoll said.

Zendric's eyes went wide. "Nahemah? She's returned?"

Kellach, Moyra, and Driskoll all spoke at the same time, finishing one another's sentences, tripping over each other's words, spilling the story of Nahemah.

Zendric listened, nodding and grunting now and then.

Kellach produced the tiny piece of the amulet. "This is all we have left. A memento."

Zendric's bushy eyebrows rose. "The Amulet of Power. Now rendered harmless! I should've known."

"Nahemah nearly succeeded in reciting the spell," Kellach said.

"But she didn't, did she? You've done well."

"Thanks." Kellach stared at his feet. Silence fell.

"You should be proud, so why the long faces?" Zendric asked.

Kellach let out a long sigh. "I wish Mom could've come back. I miss her."

"Me too," Driskoll said. "I wish I knew what happened to her."

"Me too," Moyra said softly.

Lochinvar tweeted.

"I'm sorry your mother did not return," Zendric said. "But you've overlooked something." He pointed to the shard of amulet, which began to glow around the edges.

Then, on the gem's crystal surface, Jourdain's face appeared.

She stood at a distance, then came closer, her features distorted. She smiled, and her kindness radiated out into the room. It was Jourdain, the real Jourdain, somewhere far away.

"Do not despair," she said. "One day, I will find my way home."

Then she disappeared, and the last piece of the amulet crumbled away.

Acknowledgments

Many thanks to my amazing editor, Nina Hess, and my wonderful agent, Winifred Golden. Thanks to my perceptive critiquers: Dotty Sohl, Skip Morris, Sandra Hill, Jan Symonds, Susan Wiggs, Susan Plunkett, Krysteen Seelen, Rose Marie Harris, Lois Dyer, Kate Breslin, Sheila Rabe, Janine Donoho and Pj Jough-Haan. Thanks to Byron Sacre for advice about gerunds.

MORE ADVENTURES
FOR THE

FIGURE IN THE FROST

A cold snap hits Curston and a mysterious stranger holds the key to
the town's survival. But first he wants something…from Moyra. Will
Moyra sacrifice her secret to save the town?

DAGGER OF DOOM

When Kellach discovers a dagger of doom with his own name burned
in the blade, it seems certain someone wants him dead. But who?

THE HIDDEN DRAGON

The Knights must find the silver dragon who gave their order its name.
Can they make it to the dragon's lair alive?

Ask for KNIGHTS OF THE SILVER DRAGON books
at your favorite bookstore!

For ages eight to twelve

For more information visit www.mirrorstonebooks.com

EXPLORE THE MYSTERIES OF CURSTON WITH KELLACH, DRISKOLL AND MOYRA

THE SILVER SPELL

Kellach and Driskoll's mother, missing for five years, miraculously comes home. Is it a dream come true? Or is it a nightmare?

KEY TO THE GRIFFON'S LAIR

Will the Knights unlock the hidden crypt before Curston crumbles?

CURSE OF THE LOST GROVE

The Knights spend a night at the Lost Grove Inn. Can they discover the truth behind the inn's curse before it discovers them?

Ask for KNIGHTS OF THE SILVER DRAGON books at your favorite bookstore!

For ages eight to twelve

For more information visit www.mirrorstonebooks.com

THE NEW ADVENTURES

THE DRAGON QUARTET

The companions continue their quest to save Nearra.

DRAGON SWORD
Ree Soesbee

It's a race against time as the companions seek to prevent
Asvoria from reclaiming her most treacherous weapon.

DRAGON DAY
Stan Brown

As Dragon Day draws near, Catriona and Sindri stand as
enemies, on opposing sides of a feud between the most
powerful wizards and clerics in Solamnia.

DRAGON KNIGHT
Dan Willis

With old friends and new allies by his side, Davyn must
enlist the help of the dreaded Dragon Knight.

DRAGON SPELL
Jeff Sampson

The companions reunite in their final battle with
Asvoria to reclaim Nearra's soul.

**Ask for Dragonlance: the New Adventures
books at your favorite bookstore!**
For ages ten and up.
For more information visit www.mirrorstonebooks.com

Want to know how it all began?

Want to know more about the Dragonlance® world?

Find out in this new boxed set of the first Dragonlance titles!

A Rumor of Dragons
Volume 1

Night of the Dragons
Volume 2

The Nightmare Lands
Volume 3

To the Gates of Palanthas
Volume 4

Hope's Flame
Volume 5

A Dawn of Dragons
Volume 6

Gift Set Available
By Margaret Weis & Tracy Hickman
For ages 10 and up

KNIGHTS OF THE
SILVER DRAGON™

A YOUNG THIEF.

A WIZARD'S APPRENTICE.

A 12 YEAR-OLD BOY.

MEET THE KNIGHTS OF
THE SILVER DRAGON!

SECRET OF THE SPIRITKEEPER
Matt Forbeck

Can Moyra, Kellach, and Driskoll unlock the secret of the
spiritkeeper in time to rescue their beloved wizard friend?

RIDDLE IN STONE
Ree Soesbee

Will the knights unravel the statue's riddle
before more people turn to stone?

SIGN OF THE SHAPESHIFTER
Dale Donovan

Can Kellach and Driskoll find the shapeshifter
before he ruins their father?

EYE OF FORTUNE
Denise Graham

Does the fortuneteller's prophecy spell doom
for the knights? Or unheard-of treasure?

For ages 8 to 12

THE NEW ADVENTURES

JOIN A GROUP OF FRIENDS AS THEY UNLOCK MYSTERIES OF THE DRAGONLANCE WORLD!

TEMPLE OF THE DRAGONSLAYER
Tim Waggoner

Nearra has lost all memory of who she is. With newfound friends, she ventures to an ancient temple where she may uncover her past. Visions of magic haunt her thoughts. And someone is watching.

THE DYING KINGDOM
Stephen D. Sullivan

In a near-forgotten kingdom, an ancient evil lurks. As Nearra's dark visions grow stronger, her friends must fight for their lives.

THE DRAGON WELL
Dan Willis

Battling a group of bandits, the heroes unleash the mystic power of a dragon well. And none of them will ever be the same.

RETURN OF THE SORCERESS
Tim Waggoner

When Nearra and her friends confront the wizard who stole her memory, their faith in each other is put to the ultimate test.

For ages 10 and up

4 ordinary girls
+ 4 mysterious messages
+ 4 crazy dares
= a whole lot of fun!

Nova Rocks!

Nova learns to follow her own dreams of becoming a rock star
without breaking her mom's heart.

Carmen Dives In

When Carmen follows her mystery message, she discovers there
may be more to her cheerleading stepsister than meets the eye.

Bright Lights for Bella

A mystery message helps Bella overcome her fear before she
stars in the school play.

Rani and the Fashion Divas

Rani takes a chance and she finds something she never
expected: a true friend.

Do a dare, earn a charm, change your life!

Ask for Star Sisterz books at your favorite bookstore!

For more information visit www.mirrorstonebooks.com